Murder at Catmmando Mountain, Georgie Shaw Cozy Mystery #1

ANNA CELESTE BURKE

Murder at Catmmando Mountain
Copyright © 2016 Anna Celeste Burke
www.desertcitiesmystery.com

Cover Design by Anna Celeste Burke
Public Domain Photo from Pixabay.com

ISBN-13:978-1530456215
ISBN-10:1530456215

DEDICATION

To women who discover that their work, at a theme park or elsewhere, makes them "accidental sleuths" in so many ways!

Books by USA Today Bestselling Author, Anna Celeste Burke

Murder at Catmmando Mountain, Georgie Shaw Cozy Mystery #1

Love Notes in the Key of Sea, Georgie Shaw Cozy Mystery #2

All Hallows' Eve Heist, Georgie Shaw Cozy Mystery #3

A Merry Christmas Wedding Mystery #4

Murder at Sea of Passenger X, Georgie Shaw Cozy Mystery #5

Murder of the Maestro, Georgie Shaw Cozy Mystery #6 [2017]

~~~~~

Cowabunga Christmas, Corsario Cove Cozy Mystery #1

Gnarly New Year, Corsario Cove Cozy Mystery # 2

Heinous Habits, Corsario Cove Cozy Mystery #3

Radical Regatta, Corsario Cove Cozy Mystery #4 [2018]

~~~~~

A Dead Husband Jessica Huntington Desert Cities Mystery #1

A Dead Sister Jessica Huntington Desert Cities Mystery #2

A Dead Daughter Jessica Huntington Desert Cities Mystery # 3

A Dead Mother Jessica Huntington Desert Cities Mystery #4

A Dead Cousin Jessica Huntington Desert Cities Mystery #5 [2018]

~~~~~

Love A Foot Above the Ground Prequel to the Jessica Huntington Desert Cities Mystery Series

CONTENTS

ACKNOWLEDGMENTS

Thanks to Vic, a devoted husband and first reader of all my books!

I'm grateful for Ying Cooper's assistance reediting this book as a stand-alone novella and as the first book in the box set, Georgie Shaw Cozy Mystery Series: Novellas 1-3.

Feedback from cozy mystery fans who have had kind words to say about Georgie Shaw, Jack Wheeler, and Miles has been wonderful. I'm especially grateful to Peggy Hyndman for her detailed notes about this book. Thanks as well to Doward Wilson, Donna Wolz, Michele Bodenheimer, Karen Vaughan, Tara Brown, Andra Weis, Andrea Stoeckel, Karin Tillotson, Kay Sarginson, Michele Hayes, Bonnie Dale Keck, Denise Austin, Michael Benson, Lynne Moody, Bev Smith, and John Presler who read and reviewed the book.

A big thank you to those who voted for Murder at Catmmando Mountain as one of the 50 Self-published Books Worth Reading in 2016. What an honor!

1 WORKING FOR THE CAT

"It's such a marvelous world...
a MARVELOUS MARLEY world!"

Doing PR—public relations—for a cat isn't easy. Working in any capacity for a very famous cartoon cat might sound like a dream job, but it's not. The Furry Caped Avenger, Catmmando Tom, may be a superhero, but his megalomaniacal creator is an altogether different kind of character. Maximillian Marley loves animals. People, not so much, even though they're the lifeblood of Marley's pastoral theme park,

Arcadia. It's the two-legged visitors that pay the $100 admission fee for adults and $50 for children under twelve.

On occasion, their pets are welcome, too. All the enchantment produced by other divisions of Marvelous Marley World Enterprises relies on hard-earned cash people dole out. That includes visits to the Marvelous Marley World Resorts, as well as purchases of videos, movies, and merchandise featuring Marvelous Marley World characters.

As I reviewed our current PR agenda, I straightened my posture to shoulder the burden. Super cat cartoons, movies, and merchandise had made Max Marley very wealthy. A host of animated animal characters had followed on the furry heels of Catmmando Tom's acclaim. A few human characters, often cast in supporting roles, were included in the projects produced at Marvelous Max Studios. The theme parks and resorts were next. The first Arcadia was built here in Orange County, California, near our World Headquarters. Each iconic character has a special place in Arcadia Park, a fantasyland of dreams and adventures, built around relationships between super pets and their owners. In Max Marley's imagination, it wasn't always clear who owned whom, however. Most of the time his stories involved super pets rescuing their beloved humans and endangered animals from ne'er-do-wells of one species or another.

Uncle Max, as he prefers we call him, demands that his theme parks and resorts be kept in perfect order. Nevertheless, a surprising number of "faux paws," as we refer to them around here, require attention day in and day out. Inadvertent offenses to park guests, like when the beloved Sir Dartmouth the Lion-Hearted Lion bumped into a toddler, knocking him to the ground. Characters stepped on toes, whacked guests with an unguarded tail, or otherwise offended them. Birthday parties didn't always measure up to expectations. Guests panicked about stolen items that turned out not to be missing at all, or to have been lost, not stolen. Food that was too hot, too cold, or too something, required rapid intervention by park rangers. In their spiffy Legion of Purrfect Park Rescue Ranger outfits, they roamed Arcadia Park assisting guests. They were on the front lines when it came to catching problems, or when called into action by another Marvelous Marley World "family" member who spotted a problem.

Occasionally, a dysfunctional member of the Marvelous Marley World family caused a problem deliberately. Pirate Pete, a smart-mouthed parrot, had become too mouthy several times before management replaced the guy wearing the brightly colored feathered suit. The use of profanity by "associates" or "family members," as Marvelous Marley World's corporate handbook refers to employees, is forbidden in the park and resorts. A drunken Poacher Pierre, perhaps too much into the role of the bad guy character he portrayed in animated films, had gone on a bottom-pinching spree one day. It had taken a whole squad of park rangers to escort the cackling character out of the park. That had been a mess to clean up, although many of the women had been more amused than angered by the incident.

What on earth had I been thinking when I gave up my job in the Food and Beverage Division at Marvelous Marley World? All things food-related had been my first love, and I'd started working in the park as a chef, straight out of culinary school. Despite the increasing number of women training as chefs, a decidedly male-oriented culture had prevailed in the theme park and hotel kitchens. One of the worst insults meted out was, "You do that like a housewife." The statement was typically delivered by a European chef while slashing the air with a French knife for emphasis.

I loved being a chef and succeeded in working my way up to Sous Chef quickly. It's at that point I completed a degree in business administration, with a minor in communications, and made the leap from the kitchen to Food and Beverage Management. The move into management gave me the opportunity to influence the overall quality of food in the park, to oversee hiring, training, and professional development of kitchen staff, and do what I could to find creative ways to provide excellent food to the guests while heeding the constant drumbeat to cut costs.

After more than twenty-five years at the "Cat Factory," our insiders' term for the corporation founded on Catmmando Tom's success, I made another leap. The decision to move out of the Food and Beverage Division into Public Relations wasn't an easy one. What had I been thinking? For one thing: that I wasn't getting any younger. The likelihood of obtaining the senior position in the Food and Beverage Division before I retired had dimmed when I was passed over for promotion by Max Marley's daughter. Mallory Marley-Marston, in my book, bore a resemblance to Cruella de Vil, alluding to a figure from another well-known distributor of animated tales. Maybe that resemblance was because the woman hated animals and people.

Her anorectic thinness and aversion to food made it difficult to understand how she had chosen the Food and Beverage Division as her bailiwick. She spouted a lot of hooey about bringing healthy eating to the parks and resorts while claiming to have a background in nutrition. According to gossip, that "background in nutrition" came directly from lectures in rehab where she ended up after her eating disorder and pill-popping got the better of her.

More than once I had seen the pill-popping for myself. "Vitamins," she had said as she knocked back a couple during a meeting. "Allergies," she had told us at another event. At one point, during the first year of her rule, she had taken an unexpected absence. Twenty-eight days to be exact, as in rehab. It was supposed to be hush-hush, of course. But people still speculated on the timing. While the cat's away, the mice will play, so that adage goes. Those were 28 glorious days, despite the challenge of having to step in to fill her shoes without notice. Too soon, though, she was back at the helm, waving a finger in my face and speaking to me in a shrill voice. I can't remember what accompanied the finger-pointing, since all I heard was that line from the Wizard of Oz: "And your little dog too!"

I was considering early retirement when a position opened, here, in PR. Because of my minor in communications, I had been more engaged in PR than most execs in the Food and Beverage Division. For years, I had worked with key people in PR and knew what went on in the division very well. The director, Doug Addams, invited me to apply when his second-in-command made a sudden mid-career move to a "real PR firm." Doug was not unaware of my plight having dealt with Mallory-the-Worm-Hearted, as he called her, many times. He was more than happy to facilitate my move.

PR is a smaller division than Food and Beverage. The move had been a lateral one rather than a move up, but the Hallelujah Chorus had gone off in my head the day that position was offered to me. Despite the constant troubleshooting my new job involves, I am still inclined to do a little mambo whenever Doug and I leave a meeting in which Mallory is present. The absolute worst meetings are those in which her daddy was also in attendance. She affects a slight Southern drawl in his presence and a giggly, demure demeanor, with her claws and fangs retracted. The Southern accent is inexplicable, given she was brought up in Los Angeles.

"Southern California," Doug once offered with a shrug of his shoulders and a shake of his head. Even the Southern accent is easier to take than that obsequious little-girl routine.

I had just finished perusing my email, checking for any new hot spots on the "faux paws" radar, when all the trouble broke loose. My office phone rang, my smartphone pinged, an alert popped up on my desktop computer, and Doug Addams burst through my office door. He did not even knock—a breach of protocol for the oh-so-proper Director of PR.

"We've got to get to Catmmando Mountain, now! They've found a body." With that, he was gone. I grabbed my smartphone, made sure I was wearing my corporate nametag and set off in hot pursuit.

"A body—as in a human one—a real dead person?" I ran to catch up with Doug as he reached the elevator and hit the down button.

"Yes, a body. One of our maintenance guys found it and called it in. The police are on their way. Security has already shut down Catmmando Mountain Conquest and cordoned off the area. I've also sent a team from Crowd Control to set up a perimeter and redirect guests away from the scene."

2 PURRFECT MURDER

In my quarter of a century working for the Cat, a lot of things had gone wrong. Despite the perfectly created setting with flowers always in bloom, birds chirping, butterflies flitting, manicured green grass, bubbling streams, waterfalls—life happens. People stumble and fall or have some other accident. Sometimes, those accidents involved a malfunction of the Raptor Rail, the cars on the Otterbaun, the Swan Boats or Pup Wagons—any one of a dozen Arcadia Park vehicles used to transport people. Even low-tech, horse-drawn carriages aren't always safe. Live horses are unpredictable in a crowded park filled with squealing children, piped in music, toots and whistles. Accidents can happen any day with tens of thousands of people coursing through the park.

Our guests become sick, too. Folks sometimes arrive at the park sick and get sicker. Not surprising, since no one wants to disappoint kids counting on a trip to Arcadia. There have even been deaths in the park or at the resorts, typically a heart attack or stroke. This incident was the first time since I had stepped into the PR role a year ago that I was dealing with a death in Arcadia Park.

I stood next to Doug, in silence, as we rode the elevator down to the basement. He bowed his shoulders, like Atlas. A few years older than me, the sprinkle of gray in Doug's hair was usually the only obvious sign of aging. Today a cloud hovered, making the lines on his face stand out. A dead body in the magical land of Arcadia was an enormous burden—a PR nightmare, for sure.

We could have stopped at ground level. In a lovely complex of modern buildings located outside the theme park, our office building is surrounded by gardens and topiaries cultivated into the shape of our corporate cartoon characters. Other animals not yet turned into media darlings, danced and pranced among the famous Marley World figures along palm-lined streets and around fantasy fountains that adorn the World Headquarters campus. At night, the whole setting sparkles with twinkle lights, and the fountains cast off a colorful display.

From ground level, we could have walked to a tram station, then hopped on the Raptor Rail and ridden to the park. The sleek monorail, embellished with the likeness of the Golden Eagle, was swift and could have taken us to the main gate in minutes. At this hour, that could be a mob scene. Instead, we opted to go underground. A golf cart would allow us to make our way through a network of underground tunnels, on a more direct route to Catmmando Mountain.

Yes, there are tunnels beneath Arcadia Park and the surrounding corporate buildings—just like that other well-known theme park located in Florida. We didn't use the "D-word" often. Mention of Disney was about as upsetting to Max Marley as the use of profanity. Not that he always avoided the use of four-letter words himself. Given his paternalistic managerial style, it was a "do as I say, not as I do" kind of rule.

That applied as well to references to Disney. If Uncle Max drew a comparison to Disney films, parks or resorts—usually a negative one—it was okay for him, though not for us.

Doug drove as quickly as he dared through the maze of tunnels, without endangering associates headed to or from locker rooms where they changed into their park "outfits," as we called the ensembles they wore. "Outfits, not uniforms," Marvelous Marley World's Associates' Handbook read, "because here at Marvelous Marley World, we're all outfitted with all we need to provide the best service and assistance to our cherished guests."

My unusually taciturn boss slowed down and honked when he came to a blind corner. As he made a right turn, he was forced to come to a complete stop. A shepherdess, with her pantaloons exposed, had hiked up the hoop on her skirt. She finished whatever adjustment she was making and scrambled to retrieve the lovely shepherd's crook that had fallen to the ground before we could run it over. That was fortunate because that shepherd's crook is a technological wonder, with the capacity to deliver special effects.

"Oh my, I'm so sorry," she said, in a sweet voice indicating that she was already "in character." The Heidi-like shepherdesses were a favorite among the park guests. This one was near perfect. Not only in voice but in her make-up and a wig of ringlets she straightened just a tad as she smoothed her skirt.

The tunnels and other areas "backstage" are used to do just what Giselle, as her nametag noted, was doing—making sure her appearance was perfect, so nothing detracted from the role she played once she was in the park. When she rode up the elevator, she would emerge from a hidden doorway ready to mingle with adoring fans. Giselle, not her real name, of course, would smile and swish and twirl through the crowd until she took her mark at a predetermined spot. There she would sing one of several Marvelous Marley chart-topping hits from the shepherdess series of movies featuring not just Giselle, but Arielle and Laurielle, too. The shepherdesses were among the human characters who worked alongside all the animate and inanimate animals embodying interspecies friendship, stewardship, rescue, and protection themes evident everywhere you went in Arcadia Park.

There's nothing natural about Max Marley's coloring book version of nature. Unblemished by weeds or dirt, the surroundings have a "Land of Oz" ambiance. Arcadia is colorful, with Hobbit-like habitats in lush gardens, treehouses filled with audio-animatronic birds, idyllic small-town storefronts, fantasy cottages, hedgerows, and lollypop trees. The lines blur between the real and the fanciful. Because of the underground tunnels, guests never see any delivery trucks in the park. No garbage trucks or dumpsters, either. Associates whisk garbage away via an automated vacuum collection system, part of the underground city of utility corridors. A horde of groundskeepers and maintenance workers tend to paradise before and after the park closes, sometimes working under bright lights to do that at night.

The Wild Kingdom eat-or-be-eaten theme that pops up on nature shows does not appear anywhere in Arcadia Park, although burgers are on menus throughout the park. As critics have pointed out—Arcadia connotes domestication—nature subjugated and controlled, rather than wilderness preserved. That's another issue guaranteed to set off Uncle Max. I take Arcadia for what it is—a fun, almost corny, tribute to pets and other animals, not nature writ large. "Mad Max," as we sometimes called him, has bigger dreams—delusions of grandeur manifested by his efforts to preserve a pastoral vision that has never existed anywhere in the real world. Needless to say, nowhere in that vision is there a place for death.

"Thanks," I hollered to Giselle, as we took off again. Doug had said nothing since we left my office.

He had a grim look on his face. "Doug, are you okay?"

"Yes, yes. I just hate it when the rumor mill gets out ahead of us after an event like this one. Park Associates found the body and should have gone into 'circle the wagons' mode immediately. That means mum's the word until we have the facts."

"That hasn't happened?"

"No," he said, as he displayed his phone. "I'm already getting emails with rumors that are going around—asking me if they're true."

"Like what?"

"Like this was no accident. The woman found at the base of Catmmando Mountain was murdered. Not only do they know that an attack occurred at Catmmando Mountain's, but someone's circulating incredibly insensitive social media copy about 'the purrfect setting for a purrfect murder,' if you can believe it."

"Geez Louise," I said. "How could they know that unless they were at the scene?"

"My point exactly. The information must be coming from an insider which means we've got a leak."

My mind began to race, and I felt a pit open up in my stomach. The only thing I could imagine that was worse than death in the park was a murder. No wonder Doug was white-knuckled as he drove the golf cart.

"I suppose someone could have overheard the team members talking among themselves. News like that would travel like wildfire," I muttered.

"Yes, as insensitive as it is, that tagline about Murder at Catmmando Mountain is a perfect sound bite, isn't it? On Valentine's Day, no less! Not good. Let's hope it doesn't turn out to be some crime of the heart—a lover's quarrel taken to the extreme."

"Yikes! The media would have a field day with it, given all the promotion we've done for our 'Love is Purrfect in Arcadia Park' holiday theme." I tried to think of something reassuring to say. Murder resulting from a lover's quarrel was bad, that's true. Would it be any better if this turned out to be a mugging or a random murder committed by a psycho killer on the loose in Arcadia Park?

"Doug, I don't think we should get ahead of the facts. Whatever's going on, we'll deal with it. Once we've determined guests in Arcadia park are safe, we'll handle the PR fallout. You know how short the news cycle is, no matter what's happened. We'll come up with counter-measures. There are always so many good things going on at Arcadia Park that we'll be able to shift the focus to those."

Rolling out the hearts and flowers stories from Arcadia Park was our forte in the PR Department. Not just on Valentine's Day. Stories of people and their pets are a mainstay of Arcadia Park's positive message. A portion of the proceeds from admissions goes to no-kill shelters. Twice a year the park sponsors free pet care days where mobile vet hospitals offer essential services for free—like spaying or neutering, immunizations, and tagging pets. Arcadia Park hosts an annual pet show, too.

Several romance themed messages were in the works today.

Those stories were part of an ongoing campaign to portray the park as a lovely setting for guests with more in mind than fun for kids. A "Bring your Valentine" Couples Rate was in effect for the day—two admissions for the price of one. Roving reporters would snap photos of lovers strolling hand-in-hand, buying roses for each other, or having their picture taken in front of a giant heart-shaped garland of flowers at Swan Lake. More than once, that spot had been chosen for a proposal of marriage—borrowing a moment from one of the more romantic movies, The Swan Prince's Bride, in Marvelous Max Studios film archives. The swan boats glide through a modern-day tunnel of love, where the story of the sad Swan Prince who finds his soulmate plays out in a series of stunning tableaus that inspire proposals. After a death in the park, especially if it turned out to be murder, all those soft, sentimental stories would seem insensitive.

"Maybe I should put a hold on the distribution of *Valentine's Day Love Notes from the Park*—just until we know more," I suggested.

"Yeah, that's a good idea. Send a message to Kelly, if you don't mind."

"Will do." I texted Kelly Larson, Doug's executive assistant, and asked her to have all Valentine Notes held until after lunch. Next, I sent a text to my administrative assistant, Carol Ripley. "I've got Carol pulling together a crisis team meeting for us this afternoon, Doug." I searched Twitter and saw tweets, dang it, featuring hashtag #Arcadiatroubles. Fortunately, there was no word yet about a dead body, and not so many tweets that the news about Arcadia Park was trending.

"Glad you're thinking! Clearly, I'm not at the top of my game."

"I'm sorry you're taking this so hard, Doug. None of this is your fault—

even if there has been a leak or the guys haven't done a stellar job at containment. The timing stinks, given it's a holiday."

"There is another rumor, Georgie." My name is Georgina—a last minute choice because my parents had gone to the delivery room believing they were having another boy. Everyone calls me Georgie and that's fine with me.

When I was growing up, the name got me unwanted attention at times, but I liked the balance it brought to my sense of self. Georgina was rather regal and very girlish while Georgie seemed more down-home and made me feel more like one of the guys. I had lots of male friends, in addition to three older brothers. That has come in handy more times than I can count. Being able to hang around men without always feeling the need to defer or flirt has proved critical as I climb the ranks in management.

"So, Doug, are you going to tell me the other rumor?"

Doug pulled into a parking spot beside another golf cart, shut it off and looked straight at me. "The woman is someone we know." Without another word, we hopped from the vehicle and headed to a nearby elevator. In less than a minute, the elevator delivered us to Catmmando Square, with Catmmando Mountain and Fortress Friendship looming. The doors shut behind us. The doors painted to blend into the building's façade were no longer visible to passersby once they closed.

"No more rumors, Doug. Let's find out for ourselves."

3 PURSILLA'S PANIC

Doug and I stepped out of the elevator onto the corner of Catmmando Boulevard and Shepherdsville Road. Each pedestrian roadway in Arcadia Park is paved in a different color and stamped in a distinct pattern for each area of the park. A kind of "Follow the Yellow Brick Road" strategy, it's intended to help guests navigate the park. Doug made a beeline across the road, heading for the lead member of the containment crew. His team was busy cordoning off a playground and picnic area adjacent to Catmmando Mountain. Portable partitions were being put up to block the view of whatever was going on in there. A man of medium height and build, in a dark brown suit, stepped out from behind one of those partitions and held out his hand to Doug. I'd taken two steps in their direction when a woman's shrieks stopped me in my tracks.

"Argh! Cruella—it's Cruella!" Those shrill cries came from a large, white, fluffy Purrsilla, Catmmando Tom's lady friend in his cartoon adventures. She rushed toward me in a blind panic. The plush tail that towered above her head was pinned to her body so she could move quickly. That's a no-no for anyone playing the role since the luxurious tail is Purrsilla's most attractive feature. Apart from the gorgeous green, heavily-lashed cat eyes, anyway. Under normal circumstances, a park ranger would have taken her aside. Today everyone was distracted. Including me, given the shocking claim Purrsilla was making as she skittered my way. I snagged her before she could run headlong into a throng of guests.

"Whoa, Purrsilla, slow down!" I didn't exactly grab her by the scruff of her neck, but close. It took some doing to hang on to her. I'm strong, thanks to regular workouts. She was terrified, and her first inclination was to swat at me with a big paw—also a no-no in the associate handbook for those charged with bringing Marvelous Marley World's beloved character to life.

"Stop, Purrsilla. Take a deep breath, and, please, lower your voice." She let go of her tail which almost whopped me in the face as it sprang back into place. Then she buried her big cat head into her oversized paws. I tried patting her on the back, hoping to calm her.

"She's okay, folks. Sorry for the trouble." That dispersed the crowd that had gathered. Still hanging onto her, I walked Purrsilla toward the doors that led backstage. Doug and that man in the brown suit were eying me. I waved off Doug.

"Purrsilla's just fine," I called out loud enough for Doug and anyone else still standing around to hear.

Doug waved in return.

"Who's inside there?" I whispered. Calling her Purrsilla wasn't going to cut it if I wanted to reach the human having a meltdown. I hit a spot on the wall, and those hidden doors opened. Once we were underground, Purrsilla removed the top of her costume.

"I'm so..." she hiccupped, "sorry. It was horrible. I lost it. Cruella's dead!" The young woman who still had not told me her name reached out and grabbed me with those paws and sobbed on my shoulder.

"Are you talking about Mallory

Marley-Marston?" I felt a shimmy of fear run down my spine. *Someone we know*, Doug had said.

"Yes. We called her Cruella de Vil. I know we shouldn't have done that, but it fit. She was a mean person—always giving my friends who work in Snappy Treats a hard time. Nothing was ever good enough for that hag! They just hated her, and so did I," she gasped. "Oh no! I don't mean we hated her enough to do that to her—kill her! Who could do that to anyone?"

"It's going to be all right. Uh, I'm sorry, I still don't know your name."

"Debbie. Debbie Dinsmore."

"Don't worry, Debbie." I looked around to make sure we were alone, lowered my voice to a conspiratorial level. "A lot of us called her Cruella." *Or worse*, I thought. Debbie let out a huge sigh of relief. "I'm sorry you had to see her... had to see anyone in that condition. You need to put your feet up in the break room. Calm your nerves and then go home."

"But my shift's not over for hours. I just came on duty..." Another round of sobbing cut off her words.

"No problem. We're going to shut down much of this area for a while. I'll fix it with your supervisor, Megan Donnelly, okay?" Debbie nodded in agreement. "Does she know how to reach you later?"

"Yes," Debbie said with a puzzled look on her face.

"Good! I'm going to have her call you with a referral for someone to speak to about what you witnessed today." Her puzzled expression morphed into wariness. "Trust me. It'll help—I went through something like this myself— years ago. I should have talked to someone right away. The company will pay for it, and we'll cover a few days paid leave if you want to take it." She didn't respond one way or the other. What had she seen? I uttered a silent prayer that whoever had leaked information about what was going on also hadn't taken pictures.

"I'm calling Megan right now. You have to promise me you'll calm down and that you'll see the person Megan finds for you, please?"

"Sure. I do need to take the day off. Talking to somebody couldn't hurt." She rubbed tears from her face with a paw—no-no number three, but who was counting on a day like today?

Megan picked up my call on the first ring. I filled her in on the situation. Not that I knew much myself.

I must have conveyed the seriousness of the matter because Megan sprang into action and insisted that Debbie stay with me. She planned to escort the young woman to the break room where she could change.

Then she would transport Debbie to a pick-up spot where a company driver would take her home. I was impressed by Megan's willingness to put herself out there for an associate. As Arcadia Park Operations Officer, staff management was an important part of her job. Not all she had to do, however, as she often pointed out when griping about her workload. Park Operations did involve a lot of duties besides managing associates. It included finances, health and safety, and guest relations, too. In no time at all, Megan arrived in a golf cart.

"Thanks, Megan, you're on the ball! That was fast."

"No problem. I take my job seriously." As she spoke, she stepped out of the golf cart and guided Debbie around to the passenger seat. Megan dabbed at her face with a tissue, before climbing back into the driver's seat. "I moved a little too fast and scraped my face when I jumped into the golf cart. See you later, Georgie." Megan left as quickly as she had arrived.

Once Megan had Debbie squared away, I had no choice but to go back out into Arcadia Park and face whatever had sent Purrsilla running away in terror. No screaming characters when I stepped out of the elevator this time, but plenty of noise, and activity everywhere.

People were streaming from Catmmando Mountain Conquest, a roller coaster thrill ride that took guests at breakneck speed through twists and turns inside and outside the massive mountain located in the center of Arcadia Park. Still whooping and hollering, riders blinked as they came to a stop. The last segment of the Conquest raced through the dark as Catmmando Tom battled evil-doers around them. Explosions lit up the darkness. Objects hurtled toward them in 3D, before Tom and his crack team won the day. In a cascade of fireworks and Catmmando Tom's triumphant anthem, guests blasted out into the bright California sunshine once again. Crowd Control had roped off exit lanes leading guests off of the thrill ride and away from that dead body by the most direct route possible.

The scene of the crime, as they say on all those cop shows, was now well-contained. Those shields encircled the perimeter, and Park security guards stood watch at the opening. A swarm of people were moving about, but there were no flashing police sirens or lights— no police cars or rescue vehicles at all. Two uniformed police officers stood with our security team members at the entry point. I walked over and gave them my name, explaining I was with Doug. A guard noted my name in a log and moved aside so I could enter.

County   CSIs—crime   scene

investigators—as I could tell from the equipment they had with them, were working quickly on several fronts. Some were taking pictures and others making measurements, while their gloved associates collected evidence. A woman who had to be the County Coroner bent over a body. I tried not to look at what she was doing or at the figure she was examining. Instead, I headed to where Doug was standing—off to the side, speaking to the same man in the brown suit I'd seen earlier.

"How's Purrsilla?" Doug asked.

"Better. Her supervisor will make sure she gets home safe. We'll follow up with her later. I've asked them to keep this quiet until we can sort out what's gone on here. What has gone on, Doug? Purrsilla claims it's Mallory—is that correct? How did she find that out?" I realized I was pelting Doug with questions. The gentleman standing beside him peered at me; his head cocked to one side.

"Meet Homicide Detective Jack Wheeler, Georgie. Jack, this is Georgina Shaw, Assistant Director of the PR Division. We all call her Georgie. You should, too, if you want to stay on her good side."

I mustered a smile, grateful that Doug could jest though he still wore that "hand-slammed-in-a-car-door" expression on his face.

"Nice to meet you, Detective Wheeler," I said.

"Likewise, but if I'm going to call you Georgie, you need to call me Jack." A smile spread across the man's face, softening the lines that age and a whole lot of days like this one must have put there. His eyes drew me in more than his smile. There was depth in them, as you might expect from a fifty-something homicide detective who's witnessed the worst in humans. More surprising to me was his steely vibrancy with no hint of cynicism or despair.

"Will do, Jack," I said, shaking the hand he offered. Then, the oddest thing happened. I heard a funny sound in my head as he grasped my hand. Snap, crackle, pop, or something like that. I let go of his hand, but held his gaze a moment longer, wanting to hang on to the sturdiness he exuded. How did men like Jack Wheeler deal with murder and mayhem and still seem like such solid citizens? Doug's voice interrupted my reverie.

"Jack's trying to help us figure out what's happened. He can fill you in."

"I can tell you what we know so far, which isn't much. We have a lot of work ahead of us. What I can say at this point is that, yes, it's Mallory Marley-Marston. She was murdered—stabbed many times. I could be wrong, but I'm guessing whoever committed such a vicious attack had a personal grudge against the woman. Do you have any idea who might have had it in for Ms. Marley-Marston?" My head spun as I tried to make sense of the fact that Mallory was dead and struggled to respond to the detective's question. Images of almost everyone I knew at the office passed through my mind.

"She was a nasty, unhappy woman. I can't think of a single soul who could abide her. That's not to say I know anyone who disliked her enough to kill her. Nor do I know much about her personal life, other than tabloid gossip and the fact that her father is the founder of Marvelous Marley World Enterprises." He watched me intently as I uttered those words. I felt uncomfortable about speaking ill of the dead, but it was the truth—as I saw it, at least. I met his gaze.

"Give it some thought, please, and make me a list of the people who disliked her. I'm asking Doug and others to do the same. Maybe if we cross-reference the lists, one or two names will stand out. It's a break for all of us that the groundskeepers were in this location early. Probably not long after she was killed, according to the coroner. They called it in, and your team went into action before too many people could tramp through here and destroy any evidence left behind by the killer," Jack said.

"Unfortunately, we didn't act quickly enough. Purrsilla found out it was Mallory because she cut through the picnic area before we closed off access from the tunnels on that side." Doug gestured toward the back of the picnic area close to another of those hidden entrances to the underground tunnels.

"Nice job handling that big white cat's freak-out. You must have done some fast talking to calm her down and get her out of the way like that." The detective was peering at me again as he spoke. I found it disconcerting.

"Thanks, but what else was I going to do besides talk fast and act quickly to get her backstage? Slapping her across the face like they do in the movies doesn't work so well in the real world—especially when that face is hidden behind an enormous polyurethane mask." As I spoke, the detective's brow furrowed. Had I sounded snippy?

"Georgie's not big on receiving compliments. I'm not sure why—a little-red-hen, self-reliant streak. Just doing her job, even when she's doing it well, doesn't warrant praise, right Georgie?" Doug had a knowing grin on his face. Nabbed! I don't mind doling out praise to others for a job well done, but I do have a problem accepting it. A shrink I saw after a devastating personal loss years ago called it "counter-dependency"—an unwillingness to trust or depend on others.

"Doug's right. I should have just said thanks. So, thanks."

"Since you're being polite, I'll tell you that I especially liked the grab you made for the big white cat before she plowed into a bunch of kids. Nice move!" He was smiling now—testing me a little, I think.

"I *am* just doing my job, but thanks again."

Doug shrugged in a "told you so way." The detective shifted gears, as he got back down to business. Unpleasant business, by the glance Jack exchanged with Doug.

"I hate to ask you to do this, but I need you to look at something."

I gulped, recalling the mad dash Purrsilla had made. I wanted to say no. Instead, I nodded and followed the detective. Doug made no move to go with us. We walked a few yards toward a scene that was buzzing with activity. Markers had been set out, photos were being snapped, and gloved officers were collecting items and putting them into an assortment of containers.

There, sprawled out on the ground, lay Mallory. I felt faint. I couldn't recall having seen a dead body before, except at a funeral. Nothing so brutal—this was far more gruesome than the corpses on Murder She Wrote or Monk. Worse even than one of those CSI shows. A sense of unreality about it kicked in—perhaps a natural defense mechanism had been triggered. Or some mental safeguard put up long ago in reaction to that past trauma in my young life. I hadn't seen the dead body back then. At least as far as I could remember, and I'd tried mightily over the years to recall what had happened.

"You're right! Someone had it in for Mallory." I didn't even realize I'd spoken those words aloud, so I jumped out of my skin when Jack responded.

"We call that overkill." He reached out and placed a firm hand on my arm, perhaps to steady me, as he pointed out an item on the ground with a numbered tag next to it. "That's what I wanted to ask you about before we take it into evidence. Have you ever seen it before?"

"Why yes, of course—it's mine!" That woozy, out of body feeling flooded me again. "What's going on?" I asked in a bewildered tone as we walked away from the awful scene at the foot of Catmmando Mountain.

"I have no idea yet, but I intend to find out." As he spoke, he eyed me in a way that made me feel a little like a specimen under a microscope.

"The sooner, the better, if you don't mind," I added. "The idea that someone capable of 'overkill' is roaming around Marvelous Marley World is terrifying. And quit looking at me as if you're trying to picture me with a knife in my hand. I didn't do it!"

"That's what they all say," Jack responded with a grin that I hoped meant he was kidding.

Who did do it? I wondered, trying to imagine anyone I knew wielding a knife or any other weapon that could have been used to kill Mallory.

"Oh, shoot! Now you've got me doing it," I said, shaking my head to make those pictures go away.

"Welcome to my world, Georgina Shaw!"

4 CHARACTER PROBLEMS

"Dale," I said, speaking in a firm tone and trying to make eye contact with the guy in a Catmmando Tom suit standing in my office. "I appreciate the gesture, but I can't accept your dinner invitation."

I still felt shaken, as I had all day long, by the horrible scene this morning, including the fact that my gorgeous cashmere scarf had been lying in a pool of blood not far from Mallory's dead body. I'd been going over the whole dreadful scene again in my mind when Catmmando Tom barged in. Jack

Wheeler had seemed to believe me when I told him I had no idea what my scarf was doing there.

I'd done my best to answer his questions. No, I hadn't noticed that it was missing. Yes, I was pretty sure I knew when I had last worn it—about a week ago, to a large meeting of company staff. I remembered the situation because Mallory had poked at me with one of her bony fingers as I removed the scarf.

"Versace, right?" she'd asked. When I replied yes, she'd issued a nasty follow up. "How much are we paying you people in PR, anyway? I'll have to talk to Daddy about that." With that, she swished away on sky-high heels, tsk-tsking as she tossed her head and flipped her hair. Thanks to that gruesome scene in the park, I now knew she'd worn a wig that day! A similar one had come off during the struggle, revealing a head covered with nothing but tufts of hair.

Thinking back on that confrontation and her snide remarks, I couldn't remember seeing my scarf after that. I'd put my scarf on the same hanger as my coat, tucking it part way into one sleeve. By the end of the day, it had warmed up. I'd grabbed my coat but hadn't bothered to put it back on when I left the retreat. Had the scarf still been with it? I couldn't say for sure, especially there at the scene when Jack asked, and I was feeling so disconnected and light-headed. I'd promised the detective I would try to remember, once my poor trauma-addled brain settled down.

Fat chance that was going to happen anytime soon. My recollections of that unfortunate episode with Mallory revved me up even as I considered the long list of people with an axe to grind with Mallory. If I were Jack, I'd put me at the top of the list. Not just because they had found my scarf at the scene, but because Mallory had taken the top spot I coveted in the Food and Beverage Division. My aspiration to hold that position was no secret. Nor had I hidden the fact that I disliked working for Mallory. Her comments about my scarf weren't the only public remarks that revealed her antagonism toward me, either. The fact that the murder had taken place before Arcadia Park was open for business pointed to an insider.

As a single woman, who made coffee, fed the cat, dressed for work and commuted alone, there wasn't anyone to vouch for my whereabouts this morning. In my defense, I'd like to think that if I took up homicide to advance my career, I'd have the good sense not to leave my belongings behind. Why not just leave my business card and the murder weapon, too? Stabbing Mallory twenty or more times wouldn't have been my modus operandi. Poison would have been much tidier and involved less drama. With all the little pills she carried around, it wouldn't have been too hard to make it look like an overdose.

It had been almost lunchtime when I returned to my office, but I was in no mood to eat. Instead, I drank vitamin water, more coffee, and got to work. There had been a lot to do in the wake of this tragedy, apart from my personal concerns. I put together a brief statement as a press release. Doug would deliver a similar message at a press conference scheduled for later in the afternoon. I also developed a set of talking points he could use to respond to questions from reporters. I hoped Doug could handle the job. He was a wreck.

I handed out those documents at our crisis team meeting for review and used them to get us all on the same page in case one of us got cornered by the press. "No comment" was always a good play, too, along with a referral back to Doug or me. Together we outlined a plan to deal with the fallout from what the press had, indeed, already headlined as "Murder at Catmmando Mountain." No, make that "Grisly Murder at Catmmando Mountain."

Details had leaked out about how gruesome the murder had been. Information that the victim of the crime was a high-ranking, much maligned senior female executive at Marvelous Marley World had also found its way into the hands of the press. Mercifully, the media had agreed to withhold the name, pending notification of family. Not a word, yet, from Max Marley about the death of his daughter. I felt sorry for the guy, but anxious, too. He was such a loose cannon and always unpredictable! I could imagine the man reacting with dignity, asking the public for space to deal with the loss. On the other hand, it wouldn't surprise me if he had a very public meltdown—a crying jag or a tantrum haranguing the press or the police for some imagined misdeed.

We spent a little time at our crisis team meeting trying to guess who had fed information to the media, but eventually, we gave up. That was the least of our worries. Besides, after a huge, white Persian cat character ran from the area screaming, "Cruella! It's Cruella!" it wouldn't have taken much digging to put two and two together. Mallory did not keep a low profile, and she made no more effort to court favor with the press than with anyone else. Members of the media might have noticed her resemblance to that cartoon villainess on their own.

Doug worried me. He should have stepped up to the plate and taken the lead managing this fiasco. Instead, he was distracted, said little, and let the rest of us struggle on. During that meeting, members of the team paused several times, waiting for his input. I tried to cover for him by jumping into those awkward pauses and asked the rest of our team to bear with us, given the shocking scene we had witnessed.

When Catmmando Tom waltzed into my office late in the day, unannounced, I wanted to toss him out on his oversized feline ear. This impromptu visit was not the first time Dale Kinkaid had put me in an awkward situation. He had retired early and started working as Catmmando Tom to supplement his pension. Or so he said. I figured he was just lonely. That's why I'd tried to soften my rebuffs of past invitations for more than business socializing. Today, Valentine in hand, he had crossed the line by asking me out to dinner. I was too worn out from my close encounter with the dark side to mince words, so I bluntly refused.

"I don't get it—I'm not that much younger than you. What's five years or so at our ages?" He removed the big cat head as he asked that question.

"More like ten years. That's not the

point. I don't date men from work. Period! You know that's company policy. Even if it wasn't, I'm not comfortable mixing my personal and professional lives."

"You go out with employees for happy hour all the time."

"Associates, Dale, we're all associates. I enjoy our friendship, Dale, and the time we spend with others socializing as a group at company events."

Uncle Max encouraged get-togethers and sponsored regular social events throughout the year. Departments rotated planning and organizing happy hours, too. All of that was still about business: building camaraderie, boosting morale and celebrating milestones. Anything beyond that was a problem—a problem of character or the lack thereof! Right now I faced an altogether different *character problem*, pun intended. The human part of Catmmando Tom stood staring at me in a way that made me feel vaguely uneasy, like prey.

I was trying to figure out what to say next when Carol rapped on my open door. She saw me standing by my desk in the stance I adopt when I'm about to walk someone out. That's a polite way to get a person to leave. It's a tip I'd picked up in an executive development session years ago, and it works like a charm, usually. She must also have picked up on the tension in the room. Carol eyed me and then Dale, before settling on that tiny gold box of chocolates and large, red envelope on my desk. Valentine's Day gifts from Dale that accompanied his dinner invitation.

"Uh, sorry to barge in, but you have a visitor. His name is Detective Wheeler. He doesn't have an appointment, but he says it's important." Dale had not moved a muscle until Carol mentioned Detective Wheeler's name. I saw a sudden jolt of annoyance, or maybe even dread, cross Dale's face.

"I should go. You can keep the chocolates and the card—friend-to-friend, okay?"

"Sure. I'm glad to accept them, friend-to-friend. Thanks." My "thanks" was more about the fact that he'd agreed to leave. I felt relieved by that peaceful end to what had become a tense interaction. Carol moved to my side, clearing the doorway to make room for Dale to exit.

"Aw, meow," Carol whispered under her breath in mock pity as Catmmando Tom left. She made a little clawing gesture at his back. Her dislike surprised me. This incident with Dale wasn't the first time she had been there when I tried to deflect Dale's interest, so maybe she was fed up, too. He shuffled his feet as he left, chin to his chest, with the enormous Catmmando Tom head dangling at his side.

Once in the hall, he reassembled his costume just as Jack Wheeler came around the corner. They almost collided before the detective stepped aside. That got Jack a two-fingered Catmmando Tom salute from Dale as he left, his cape catching a bit of a breeze from an open window or a fan. Detective Wheeler turned to watch the character exit. Then he shook his head and turned back toward me.

"Have you got a minute, Ms. Shaw?" As he spoke, Jack gave me the once-over. Despite the efforts to end the catcalls and unsolicited input about our bodies, men still act that way. It bothers me sometimes, but there was more appreciation than evaluation in Jack's gaze. Besides, who was I to object? I found myself doing it too—taking in the man from head to toe. Carol did not miss the exchange.

"Meeeeooww," she whispered again—almost as a purr this time. I snapped out of it, gave a barely perceptible nudge meant to shush her, and went back into corporate exec mode. That included a step behind my desk, putting more distance between the handsome homicide detective and me. I didn't stop checking him out, though. A touch of grey at his temples gave him an air of authority that went well with a firm jaw, regular features, and dark eyes. Those eyes glinted with good humor and curiosity. After a day like today, I couldn't imagine how that was possible, but it was contagious. I felt the burdens of the day lift.

"Yes, Detective, please have a seat. Carol said you needed to speak to me. I had to wrap up a previous meeting." I glanced down at the red envelope and ribbon-wrapped gold box in the middle of my desk. Awkwardness returned. A smile appeared on the detective's face.

"I was willing to wait my turn, but then I figured I'd better see for myself whether you were in or not. Carol strikes me as an excellent administrative assistant, skilled at running interference for you. You wouldn't believe how many times I get ditched by corporate bigwigs when I show up to ask questions." He winked at Carol as he spoke. She beamed back at him.

"Then I'd better get back to my desk so you two can get down to business. Would you like coffee, Detective Wheeler?" Carol asked.

"No thanks. I had a cup on the way over here."

"Well, I don't mind bringing you a cup if you change your mind." Carol brushed past the detective as he took a seat across from my desk. She paused for a second at the door and gave me a thumbs-up before shutting it.

"How can I help you?"

"I thought I might help you. Finding that scarf had to be unnerving, so I wanted to let you know that you have an alibi. You're off my list of suspects." My mouth dropped open, not sure how to take this information. Suspect? Alibi? Those words had flitted through my mind, but to hear him use them made my involvement in a murder investigation *more* stressful, not less.

"I'm sorry, but did I need an alibi?" I felt irritated by his demeanor—a little too glib. In those TV cop shows, a lot of detectives come across as surly or macho. Had my initial impression of Jack Wheeler as a stand-up guy been wrong?

"A good, solid alibi is always valuable when an item of your clothing turns up at the scene of a murder." He had a wry grin on his face. Not an expression I could describe as surly or macho, maybe a touch smug.

Hmm, what is it with this guy? I asked myself. Is he toying with me? I decided to play along. I stood there, behind my desk, and folded my arms.

"Okay, if you say so. What is it?"

"What is what?"

"What's my alibi?" I guess the abruptness of my question caught him off guard. Still, he hardly skipped a beat before answering.

"It's your FasTrak transponder. At the time your colleague was murdered, you had just sailed through one of the toll booths on your commute." I must admit I did feel a wave of relief, although I wasn't about to tell him that.

"Thanks for sharing that information. Glad you have one less suspect on your list. I'm sure you've confirmed what Doug and I told you. Mallory wasn't the most likable character in our cast of thousands, so you must have plenty of other alibis to track down." Again, he smirked. Did that count as surly or macho? Jack Wheeler was getting under my skin.

"I'm sorry if checking up on you bothers you, but that's what I do. It's my job. If it matters, I'm glad you're no longer on the list of suspects. I like it much better that way." That smirk shifted to a way more engaging smile. I tried to hold onto my stern demeanor, but it had been too long and too weird of a day. I returned the smile and sat down.

"I get it. I'm glad not to be a suspect. What I don't get, though, is how my scarf got there."

"That is a good question and another reason I'm here. Have you given any more thought about when you last saw the scarf?"

"Yes. I remember hanging it along with my coat on a rack in a cloakroom.

That was about a week ago at a site we used for a retreat."

"Who had access to that cloakroom?"

"It wasn't a 1930s nightclub—no hat check girl or anything like that. Everyone attending the retreat had access. We all just filed in there, shed our outerwear, hung it up, and left." I drummed my fingers on my desk, under his watchful gaze. "Sorry if that sounded abrupt. You may be used to this sort of horrendous situation, but I'm not."

"You never get used to horrendous situations, but I understand what you're saying." His dark eyes softened a little as he spoke, revealing what might have been a hint of sadness or weariness.

"I'm glad you understand what I'm saying because I'm not sure I do. I did have an odd interaction with Mallory that morning in which she made a nasty crack about my scarf." As I shared the details of that story, I realized how relieved I was to have that alibi. In retrospect, Mallory's threat to tattle on me to her father sounded worse than it had at the time and under the current circumstance might even be considered a motive for murder.

"So, who witnessed that interaction between you and Cruella de Vil?" Jack asked.

"You know about Mallory's nickname?"

"Geez, it was hard to miss with Purrsilla shrieking it at the top of her lungs. Doug told me it wasn't the first time he'd heard an associate use that name for Mallory. You found it an apt one for her, too, from what I understand." He wore a cat-that-swallowed-the-canary expression.

"I confess, yes. You've caught me. Does that put me back on the suspect list?"

"Nah, but it does get us back to my previous question. If there were witnesses to that cloakroom interaction between you and Cruella, it's no secret you two didn't get along and not a coincidence they chose that scarf after watching the two of you fight about it. So, who saw you and Mallory go at it and wants to frame you for her murder?"

My mouth flew open again, and I clamped it shut, setting my jaw. There was no smug look now on his handsome face. Jack was serious.

"It wasn't a fight, Jack. At least not on my part. I'm also confident that scene didn't let the cat out of the bag, so to speak. A lot of people knew one reason I'd moved to the PR Division was to get away from Mallory. There must be plenty of scuttlebutt about my dislike for her, so I'll confirm that for you. I didn't like her. But why anyone would jump to the conclusion that I wanted her dead is beyond me. At the time of our little encounter that day, the meeting was about to start, so there must have been forty people milling about as witnesses to that scene. Doug had walked into the building right before me, and Mallory had her administrative assistant, Linda Grey, with her as well as her second-in-command, Dorothy Sayers. Key people were there from other divisions, too. It's hard for me to conceive of any of them as a murderer, or angry enough with me to try to frame me."

"Desperate people will do desperate things, Georgie. Anyone willing to resort to murder to resolve a grudge or gain an objective wouldn't think twice about having someone else take the rap."

"Take the rap—you guys really talk like that?"

"You can put money on it, sweetheart," Jack replied, in a pretty good imitation of Humphrey Bogart's

Philip Marlowe. Despite my concern about being the object of a colleague's nefarious plotting, I smiled at his antics.

"I wish I could point you toward someone, but anyone at that retreat could have grabbed my scarf. Not one of whom strikes me as a murderous thug planning to kill Mallory. If that's where the killer grabbed my scarf, that implies the murder was planned and already in the works, at least a week ago, right?"

"It's possible. Not a whole lot of planning, mind you. The scene is a mess, and the attempt to implicate you amateurish. The plan must have included setting up a meeting at, or near, the spot where your colleague killed Mallory. If we're lucky, a text or email ought to give us more information about who set it up and why. Still, it's odd. If you had as many enemies as this woman had, would you agree to meet at the crack of dawn in an empty theme park?"

"I doubt her royal highness worried about it," I said. "Part of what made her so intolerable was a callous disregard for the little people in Max Marley's kingdom where she was heir to the throne. Why not ignore their hatred as well as their other sentiments that she trampled without thinking twice?"

"I suppose if she was as self-centered as you say, she might have been oblivious to threats or felt invincible. Still, if only for sheer comfort and convenience, why wouldn't she refuse to meet at that hour?"

"What if she was coerced into the meeting—blackmail, maybe? You might already know this," and I lowered my voice, "but there was another issue in her life: drugs. Gossip has it that Mallory was in and out of rehab. I hate to think of Arcadia Park as the scene of a drug deal that went wrong, but I suppose that's a possibility."

"We ran a background check immediately, and the rehab thing popped up. Her father confirmed it when I spoke to him. He wasn't much help identifying a suspect, though, and got all blustery about the idea she had enemies! Max Marley is not in good shape, by the way. The apple didn't fall far from the tree, did it?"

"Nope. We have a pet name for him, too—Mad Max." My admission got a head shake and a guffaw from Jack. I continued, "The man's a genius, but comes across as mad as a hatter at times. When Max becomes convinced he's right about something, he's at least as disinclined as his daughter to accept feedback. He can go pretty far off the rails before figuring out that's what he's done."

"It sounds like Max had a blind spot when it came to his daughter."

"Oh yes, and Mallory played him

like a fiddle. Her performance in the role of darling daughter, worshipping at the feet of her accomplished father, was Oscar-worthy. Behind the scenes, before I left my old job, I heard her grousing about 'that stubborn old man' more than once. Supposedly, Max bailed her out of trouble on numerous occasions, including that recent bout of rehab. You'd think that would have been a clue she wasn't Pollyanna. Blind spot, yes. Blustery and not helpful is about what I'd expect, given how distraught he must have been. Did he see his dead daughter in the park like that, Detective?"

"It's Jack, remember? No, we didn't call him to the scene. I heard he showed up later at the morgue. The guy about had a stroke from what the coroner told me. Then did what you said he might do—flew off the handle, demanding they conduct a thorough autopsy. Like he had to take command to get that to happen." Jack shook his head.

"I sound harsh telling it like it is—or was—about a dead woman and her dysfunctional relationship with her father. No parent wants to outlive a child—even one as troubled as Mallory. Issuing an order is a strategy I've seen him use before. It's one of the ways Mad Max tries to cope with difficulty. Likes to feel in control, you know?"

"I get it. Poor guy. We're moving as fast as we can to find out what happened to his daughter. If we can find her phone, it might tell us who she met with this morning. It wasn't with her at the scene. Her purse was there with a wallet, keys, and other stuff like that. No cell phone, though. It wasn't at her office when we picked up her computer. Linda Grey says there was nothing on Mallory's calendar about a meeting this morning. So far, there's nothing on her computer, either. The phone wasn't in her car, but a team at Mallory's house is still searching. We should get her phone records tomorrow. Maybe that'll give us something. Can you get me a list of everyone at that retreat when your scarf disappeared?"

"No problem. I can contact the coordinator of the event. We had to sign in, so there's an attendance record. I'm still working to put together that list of people who openly disliked Mallory. I hope that's not your go-to 'whodunit' list, since I'm on it. That and my scarf make it two strikes against me already, right?"

"Don't worry about any three-strikes-and-you're-out rule. It's way more complicated than that to figure out 'whodunit.' Besides, it would have been quite a feat to leave that scarf at the crime scene while you were on your way to work. So, one strike: motive, yes. Opportunity, no." I paused for a moment trying to figure out how worried I should be and what else I could do to move the investigation along.

"Is there anything else besides getting those lists that I can do?"

"As a matter of fact, yes. There is one more thing you could do. Let me buy you dinner." Those strange snap-crackle-pop sounds happened in my head again, as I met his dark eyes. A warm flush followed.

"No," I responded instantly. Disappointment registered on his face. I fixed that in a flash. "I will have dinner with you, but we go Dutch."

"Go Dutch? I haven't heard that expression for some time. I'm not an employee—it's not against company policy to date me, right?"

My mouth fell open for the third time, and after I'd collected myself, I asked, "Were you eavesdropping on Dale and me?"

"I'm a detective, ma'am, what can I say? I followed Carol and was about to barge in here when I realized you weren't alone. After a minute or two of listening to your anguished politeness, I thought it was time for that cad to go—super cat or no super cat." He shrugged. I pursed my lips, still not certain how to take this guy. While I was thinking, he changed the subject.

"Where do you want to go for dinner?" I was hungry—starving, in fact.

"How about the Blue Pacific? Fantastic food and they have music. Do you like jazz? I could use a little music to soothe my soul after today."

"The Blue Pacific," Jack said, letting out a low whistle. "Working for the Cat must pay well. That place is pricey. Thanks for offering to go Dutch. As for soul-soothing, I had an alcoholic beverage in mind."

"Perfect! They have an exquisite wine selection. My treat for your diligence in getting me off the suspect list so soon by finding out I have an alibi. I started here as a chef, so I'm picky about where I eat. And yes, the Cat pays well. As you can tell, I earn every penny of it."

"I won't argue with that!" Jack stood up. I did too. I grabbed my purse from a drawer at my desk. After shoving Dale's Valentine card and candy into my bag, I removed my coat from the clothes tree near the door to my office. Jack helped me slip my arms into it.

"That's odd," I said, patting one of the pockets of the coat. "I just saw my cell phone in my purse...but there's one here in my coat."

"Don't touch it! I'll bet you anything you just found Mallory's phone."

"You've got to be kidding. Am I back on the suspect list?"

5 DINNER WITH A VIEW

Two hours later, we were seated at Blue Pacific with a view overlooking the ocean and an open bottle of wine. A jazz quartet played Coltrane, the lighting low and romantic, and there I sat with a homicide detective. What a way to spend my first date in ages! If I hadn't been exhausted and freaked out, I might have been able at least to get into the film noir ambiance of the whole thing.

"Cheers!" I said, holding up my glass. Jack gave it a clink with his.

"What are we toasting?"

"That this beastly day is over, and I'm not in jail."

"I'll drink to that!" He took a sip and let out a little sigh of appreciation. "What a terrific wine. I can't imagine a better way to end a day like this one. It's a lovely view from where I'm sitting." I could tell he was talking about more than the ocean.

"Thank you. I'm glad you insisted we have dinner, despite the delay back at my office." Evidence guys had come and picked up my coat and the phone. They had gone through my things, looking for other evidence linking me to the murder. There was no sign anyone had jimmied the lock on the door, so whoever left that phone either had a key or slipped in while it was already open.

"Delay or no delay, we have to eat, even in the middle of a big case like this one."

"You may be used to dealing with

murder and mayhem. I'm not. Well, mayhem maybe, but not murder. After the first hour or so with those CSI guys, I was ready to call it a night. I'm still not feeling great about the fact that someone at the Cat Factory has made another attempt to get me to take the fall for murder."

"Cat Factory, huh? I like that. Planting the murdered woman's phone on you would have worked better if there had been texts or phone calls between you and Mallory. Whoever's behind this isn't thinking straight—not a mastermind, that's for sure. As I said before, this has been a half-baked attempt to implicate you."

"It may be half-baked, but it's unnerving, nevertheless."

"You have every right to be unnerved. Half-baked is still plenty dangerous."

"Why me? What have I done to

tick somebody off?"

"It might not be personal. The antagonism between you and Mallory is a plausible motive. That incident with the scarf was convenient—like Mallory was ramping up efforts to get you. Even if you hadn't identified that scarf as yours, a lot of other people could have done it. The very public confrontation over the scarf made that possible and drew attention to the ongoing conflict between the two of you. Murderous rivalries aren't unheard of in my business, Georgie."

"Rivalry? Mallory was daddy's girl—handpicked by Max. How could I possibly be a rival? Or anyone else, for that matter."

"Even more of a reason to get rid of her. If workplace competition is at the center of this mess, it could be personal. You may not see yourself as a formidable rival, but you are. Mad Max isn't always off the wall—you said as much. Blood may be thicker than water, but it's no substitute for cold, hard cash. He must have had some expectations that his daughter would perform adequately in that role."

"That's hard to believe. I hear what you're saying, though. Even if Max didn't want to hold her accountable, the shareholders would be after him if she screwed up too much."

"My point, exactly! I'll bet Mallory felt you breathing down her neck even after you moved to a different division. She may not have been the only one. Why not kill two birds with one stone by eliminating one rival and framing another for her murder? You're competent and experienced, poised, and attractive. Uh, sorry no compliments, I forgot." Jack sipped his wine and set the glass down. "I need to slow down—this wine is far too good."

I relished his compliments, but I'd had my shields up for so long I wasn't sure I was ready to lower them yet.

"Thanks for the kind words," I said. "I do like to hear them. I've never understood the things you're saying about such ruthless competition. Work harder. Improve yourself, yes. Murder someone to get ahead, or frame someone for murder—well, that's beyond belief. It creeps me out to think a colleague like that works at Marvelous Marley World. Even worse to find out the culprit is close enough to take my scarf and plant that phone in my coat. Close and way ahead of me, that's for sure."

"Not too far ahead. Stealing the scarf was a crime of opportunity—it required some forethought, but not a lot. Planting the phone was a little trickier. Still, you were out of your office most of the day, so any number of people could have done it. That big, obnoxious tomcat had no problem getting in there, and I barged in on you. Carol's a good assistant, but she's not on guard duty every minute."

"I agree. She's about the best administrative assistant I've ever had. I don't ask her to play guard. I prefer an open-door policy unless I'm working under a tight deadline and she knows that. It's not uncommon for colleagues to drop by without even checking in with her first. If I'm going to be away from my desk for a meeting I do shut the door, but don't always lock it. None of that is Carol's fault."

"What do you know about her, by the way?"

That question caught me off guard, despite the unpleasant realization that someone close to me was up to no good. Before I could respond, our server showed up with the appetizers we had ordered—a tiger prawn cocktail for me and crab cakes for Jack. Once the server left, I dug into that lovely cocktail, relishing the fresh, perfectly prepared jumbo shrimp. I was famished, and with an empty stomach, the wine was getting to me. The more I considered Jack's question, the more absurd it seemed.

"Do you honestly believe Carol's behind this? She's been at Marvelous Marley World a long time and has an impeccable record. She didn't like Mallory, but she hardly knew the woman. Besides, whoever killed Mallory had to have been strong, physically, right? Carol's petite, couldn't weigh much more than Mallory, and she has problems with carpal tunnel. Wouldn't all of that have given Mallory a better chance of getting away if Carol had been the one who attacked her?" Despite the rather gruesome subject matter, Jack was putting away those crab cakes.

"Excellent points. I wasn't thinking about Carol as a murderer. I wondered if she could be an accomplice—witting or unwitting. Would she have slipped that phone into your coat pocket if asked and without telling you?"

I thought about it as I ate more of my perfectly prepared shrimp. The delicious food didn't just satisfy my hunger; it comforted my restless spirit.

"Could be, if she felt convinced it was mine. Still, even if she believed it was mine, she's more likely to have put the phone on my desk along with a note that so-and-so found it. Given all that's gone on today, I can't believe she wouldn't have mentioned a stray phone turning up, even if at the time she had mindlessly slipped it into my coat pocket. She's got superb judgment when it comes to people, and being asked to do that would have registered as odd."

An image of Carol from earlier in the day popped into my head. She had been so open in expressing her sentiments about both Dale Kinkaid and Jack Wheeler. I expected frankness from her and always felt that's what I got from her—not deceit.

"It's even harder to see her as a co-conspirator in some clandestine plot to overthrow Mallory and help a colleague rise through the corporate ranks if that's where you're going with this. Too bad Carol had left by the time your guys showed up.

Ask her about it, and I'm sure she'll tell you much the same thing. She might also be better informed than I am about what's gone on in the Food and Beverage Division since I left Hurricane Mallory all to herself. You should ask Carol about that, too."

"I'm going to interview her tomorrow. And yes, when I ask Carol about how Mallory's cell phone could have ended up in your coat pocket, I'll also quiz her about what she's heard from her counterparts in Food and Beverage. I bet it hasn't been pleasant for anyone. Did your former coworkers resent you for leaving?"

"If they did, no one said so. I have no delusions about the fact that everyone who works for the Cat is expendable, so I assume my move didn't rub anyone the wrong way. I'm old enough that I could have retired instead of taking the PR position. I tried to keep Mallory in check, but there was little I could do, even as second-in-command."

I glanced at Jack, intrigued by the good-looking man seated across from me. His enjoyment of the food he was eating was apparent. There was a sensual pleasure in it that not all men exhibited. I liked that. He caught me watching him, and smiled. A thoroughly engaging smile.

Where was I? I wondered as I

tried to refocus on the question he had asked. Not easy now that his eyes had met mine. I forced myself to look away and continued, doing my best to sound businesslike.

"Besides, my departure opened a slot, allowing other people to move up. On balance, I'd say my move would have been advantageous for any number of colleagues with the ambition to climb the ladder. Dorothy Sayers took my place. She has the same haggard look on her face I wore while working for Mallory. Dorothy has never said a word to me one way or another about the job or her relationship with Mallory. Mallory's assistant, Linda Grey, has griped to Carol and me about having to run personal errands for Mallory. Linda might know more than the rest of us about how Mallory's personal and professional lives overlapped. Maybe there's something in that overlap that could help your investigation. Did Linda's irritation about being asked to fetch Mallory's dry cleaning, make her spa appointments, or feed her goldfish push her to the breaking point? I doubt it, but what do I know? As miserable as Mallory made people around her, it never crossed my mind anyone was angry enough to kill her."

"Now that she's dead, who's going to take her place?"

"No one even brought that up in our crisis management team meeting today. We had our hands full coping with the recent incident. Dorothy was there representing the Food and Beverage Division. As assistant director, she's Mallory's backup and has, no doubt, been carrying a lot of the load already. She's the most likely choice to step into the role permanently."

"Any chance they'll ask you to accept the leadership role in Food and Beverage?"

"It's possible. Like I said, we were

concentrating on getting through the day. No one has had much time to consider what Mallory's death means for the organization long term. Unless Max decides to delegate the task, he'll call the shots once he's buried his daughter and is ready to tackle business."

"So, it sounds like Dorothy Sayers is the big winner here, Georgie. With Mallory out of the way, her day-to-day life just got a whole lot better. I'll bet there's a big, fat raise to go with a permanent promotion to top dog in the Food and Beverage Division at the Cat Factory. Putting you away for the murder would guarantee they didn't give it to you. Heck, Dorothy doesn't even have to succeed in getting you charged with anything—just keep a cloud hovering over you until Max appoints her to the position permanently."

"Except that she's older than I am, Jack. I'm surprised she hasn't retired already. And, she'd have to be a sick person to do any of the things you're suggesting. I was never close to Dorothy, but she always did her job well. If you don't stay on top of them, food costs can push you into the red, fast. Dorothy was a hard worker, dependable, and good with numbers—all reasons they moved her up. Perhaps Dorothy got along better with Mallory than I did because she stayed put. Mallory was openly disdainful toward Dorothy, as she was with so many others at Marvelous Marley World. I never saw any show of resentment from Dorothy in return. It sounds like you have a lot of good questions to ask her and Linda Grey when you interview them."

"I sure do. What about that Dale Kincaid character? Was he ever alone in your office—even for a minute? It wouldn't have taken long to slip that phone into your coat pocket." Jack had stopped eating to ask that question, his fork poised to dig back in. "This is fabulous, by the way."

"I've never eaten anything here that wasn't fabulous. I'm glad you like it." I'm not sure why Jack's approval made me happy, but it did. "Dale is an odd duck—the fact that he can't take a hint, for one thing. I disliked having to lay it on the line like I did today, but he left me no choice. Perhaps it's my fault. I could have waited too long to 'just say no.' My guess is that the guy has boundary issues of his own. I'm not sure how to factor that into your theory of the murder or his role as an accomplice if he's the one who planted Mallory's phone on me. Until today, he rated only about a three on my Sludge-o-Meter. That's gone up to a six after his Valentine's Day surprise and the fact that I practically had to spell out the word 'no' for him." Jack had fixed me with an amused gaze.

"What?" I asked.

"I've heard of rating folks—the whole one-to-ten deal isn't new—but a

'Sludge-o-Meter' is one I haven't heard before. I trust your judgment as much as you trust Carol's. If you say Dale's a six, he's a six in my book."

"There is another thing. It's probably nothing, but my heightened sense of paranoia. I could have sworn Dale reacted in an uneasy way when Carol announced you were waiting to see me. I can't be sure if it was the mention of your name or the fact that a police detective was about to step into my office." I shrugged as Jack pondered what I'd told him.

"Hmm, I've already got someone checking him out. Maybe he's harmless, and it's just a coincidence he was in your office right before you found that phone, but I don't like it. If my presence made him jumpy, it could be he's had a run-in with the law. We'll see what our background check turns up. The lab will also examine that phone and your coat for prints. Although it's a long shot that there's anything for them to find. It could take a while, too, since they have their hands full with everything collected at the crime scene this morning. By tomorrow, the coroner might be able to tell us more about some of the issues you've already raised—the size and strength of the attacker, how the attack unfolded, type of murder weapon." He paused and shook his head. After pouring himself more wine, he held the bottle above my glass. I nodded, and he refilled it.

"This is a horrible conversation for a first date, isn't it? I'm sorry we had to start off like this. I should have waited to ask you out until we resolved this mess. That could take weeks or months. Frankly, I didn't want to wait that long. I'm not getting any younger, Georgie. It's not often I take to a person right off the bat." I felt a rush of compassion for the doubts he was having. I appreciated his honesty, too, and with a sudden surge of surprise I realized I was glad he hadn't waited. My shields were down after all.

"It's fine. I wish we had met under other circumstances, too. I don't date much. I don't have a lot of time to socialize outside of the workplace—and you heard my rule about that. Sixty-hour work weeks don't leave a lot of extra time for romance. It was often more hours than that while I was in the kitchen. Chefs keep odd hours and work different shifts, including nights, weekends, and holidays. I never married, though I came close once. I got used to a solitary life. My family and friends gave up asking me about my love life years ago after—oh, never mind. I won't go into all that." I leaned in and lowered my voice. "I got my AARP card in the mail this year, Jack, and I'm almost eligible to use it!"

"Now you're making me doubt your truthfulness. You don't want me to put you back on the suspect list, do you?" Jack smiled at me. I knew he was flirting, but I liked it.

"Run a background check on me. That'll prove it. How about you? Was there a Mrs. Wheeler?" He sighed and nodded yes.

"My life as a cop has been a rough one. My wife felt she had it worse than me. You've built a career for yourself. Not all women are as career-oriented or as comfortable spending so much time on their own. My wife was alone a lot while I was working my way up the ranks. I wasn't always good about checking in with her, especially in the middle of an important case. She got fed up feeling widowed before I was even dead—another worry for the wife of a homicide detective. I'm not making myself sound like good dating material, am I?"

"Marriages take two committed people to make a go of it. When it doesn't work out, it's rarely only one person's fault. It sounds to me like you've done a lot of soul-searching about what you might have done differently. Your job is what it is, as they say. I'm glad there are people like you, who can face every day what we had to face today. I couldn't do it, but I'm grateful you can. I hope I get a chance to hear more about your work—over other dinners. You can leave out the more graphic details. The puzzle-solving is intriguing, although I'd prefer not to be on the whodunit list." That brought a broad smile to Jack's face, making me think he was one of the most attractive men I'd seen in a long, long time. He reminded me of someone, an actor from old TV shows or movies. I hadn't been to a movie in months and didn't spend much time watching television either, so I couldn't place a name with the resemblance.

Our servers returned with our main course. I was grateful for the interruption. The conversation had become more intimate than I expected on a first date. Given the dire circumstances that had brought us together, I suppose it wasn't too odd that we had moved past small talk quickly.

I was still hungry enough that the aroma of my wild mushroom-crusted sea bass made my mouth water. The sizzling steak they set in front of Jack smelled delicious, too. The servers cleared away our appetizer dishes, collected the old napkins and silverware and set out new ones. With a flourish, our server presented us with fresh napkins, placing them in our laps. A second server set a new basket of warm bread on the table.

"Can we bring you anything else?"

"I'm fine, thanks," reaching for that basket of bread as I replied.

"I'm more than fine with this

incredible steak in front of me!"

"Enjoy!" With that, the server disappeared.

We dug into our food, and neither of us spoke for a couple of minutes.

"This steak is out of this world. How's your sea bass?"

"Delicious! It melts in your mouth." Jack went back to cutting his steak. Without warning, he picked up the conversation about murder and mayhem with another question.

"What about your boss, Georgie? How did he get along with Mallomar?"

"Wow, you are unearthing all our little secrets, aren't you? Fast, too!" Mallomar, like the cookie, was another name we used when talking about the woman behind her back. The name captured our disdain for Mallory's treatment of important matters as fluff.

"This is a big case with a high-profile murder victim," Jack said. "She was brutally killed in a hallowed playground for happy families. It's important to get ahead of the curve and stay there. I don't want Mad Max ranting at me, nor do I want this case to go cold. So, yes, I've made the rounds today, if only in a superficial way so far. We'll follow up with more in-depth interviews, and we'll collect formal statements from everyone who worked with Mallory. What about your boss?"

"Doug Addams has been one of my biggest supporters over the years. He knew how miserable I was once Mallory became my boss, told me about the opening, and encouraged me to apply. Once I'd done that, I heard he put in a plug for the search committee to search no further. Doug's competent and reliable—good at his job and runs a tight ship. I can't believe he'd set me up, much less that he lost his mind and murdered Mallory. He was upset, but so was I."

I flashed for a moment on how troubled Doug had been as he drove that golf cart through the tunnels this morning. Could there have been more to his distress than we all experienced learning that someone had murdered a colleague in Arcadia Park? *Stop it, Georgie,* I thought, shaking my head to clear it. Why wouldn't he have been upset since he already had an inkling that Mallory was the victim?

"I don't know how you do this. The more we talk, the more confused I become about whodunit! I'm becoming more and more paranoid, too. The fact that some maniac killed Mallory in the park points to someone on the job, but isn't there an ex-husband or a jilted lover you ought to check out, too? What if she took up with some guy she met in rehab? It could be wishful thinking, but I have no reason to regard Doug as a culprit."

"It's not only that the killer attacked her in Arcadia Park. What also has me focusing on your colleagues as culprits is the fact that someone has gone after you, too. I'm not ruling out a love affair gone wrong, a bad drug deal, or anything yet. Mallory's murder is shaping up, so far, as the work of a Marvelous Marley insider in my book." He looked directly into my eyes as he went on.

"Paranoia isn't always a bad thing. I don't want to scare you, but I do want you to be on alert. Call me, or call 911 if anything or anyone triggers your Sludge-o-Meter, promise?" The earnestness in his voice and seriousness of his gaze reached me.

"In a heartbeat," I replied. No more denial. His message had hit home.

6 CHOCOLATE POINTS

If I'd ever been more exhausted, I couldn't remember when. I felt drained from riding a roller coaster of emotions all day. Even though our dinner had started later than planned, we had lingered over coffee and the dessert, a chocolate soufflé cake. It was an indulgence, but I needed chocolate. I love chocolate, and it's a weakness, even on a good day. One reason I'd chosen the Blue Pacific was to get my chocolate fix.

Like everything else we ordered, the cake was outstanding. It's a favorite, second only to my version of the dense, flourless cake. I add vanilla, freshly made espresso from my favorite beans, and a little coffee liqueur. The alcohol bakes out, leaving a hint of something deeper than the chocolate would alone. When I let myself into the house, I was greeted with a booming "Hello" from Miles, my Siamese cat.

He's a chocolate-point, of course. When I first encountered the tiny kitten with the enormous ears, he had greeted me with several trumpet-like blasts. I named him after Miles Davis, the incredible jazz horn player. Although he's a full-grown cat now, Miles never did catch up with those ears. They're still too big for him. Miles ran to greet me, murmuring to himself. I bent to pat him on the head, and he rewarded me with loud purring. His piercing blue eyes peered up at me. I swear he can tell when I'm upset.

"Hello, Miles. How are you, Baby?

Mama's tired."

Talking to a cat, I know, is almost a cliché for a single woman of a certain age. But I don't care. Miles levitated, landing at "petting level" on the table inside the kitchen where I stash my keys and go through the mail. He got what he wanted—more petting and a smooch. His soft fur and reassuring rumbles worked to soothe away the rough edges left by the day and that warning from Jack.

I felt wary all the way home. Was I being watched? Followed? What if whoever killed Mallory decided to get rid of me, too? I drove into the garage and shut the door behind me before unlocking and exiting my car. The instant I set foot in the kitchen, I reset the alarm and sighed with relief. Jack had promised to ask for extra police patrols in my neighborhood.

Satisfied that I was okay, Miles

went into action. In a burst of energy, he did a dismount, nailed the landing, and launched into his "crazy cat" routine with his tail kinked. Miles bolted out of the kitchen, roared like a mini-lion, then leaped up and over the back of the couch, ran under the coffee table, and plopped back down at my feet, almost before I could blink. This routine was in celebration of my homecoming. One he performed nightly, it always made me laugh.

In addition to concern for my welfare and a celebratory spirit, Miles possesses a keen sense of order. He keeps me on task, anticipating where I'll go and what I'll do next. With Miles leading the way, I headed to the bedroom where I changed into pajamas. As I shed each item of clothing, I scrapped another layer of "ick" from the day. By the time I put on my soft, floral knit pajamas, I almost felt like the old me again.

Better, in fact. Jack's smile floated before me, and his hearty laugh echoed, as I fixed Miles his evening snack and made myself a cup of herbal tea. After that warning from Jack to remain alert, we stopped pondering "whodunit" and why. Dinner became more of a real date as we exchanged tidbits about our lives.

Jack and I came from very different backgrounds—me, the youngest of four children, and he, an only child. My mother was a stay-at-home mom, his, a school teacher. His dad had been a machinist, mine an accountant.

We also had some things in common. Both of us were born and raised in California. We share a love of the outdoors, although neither of us has had much time for hiking, cycling or swimming. A big fan of jazz like I am, Jack prefers the sax to a trumpet. Jack and I both enjoy theater and art as well as food and wine. I liked what I'd learned so far and felt eager to know more about him. Consequently, I did something impulsive over our decaf coffee. I invited Jack to dinner. Now I felt almost panicky. What had I done? One date and I offer the guy a home-cooked meal! Fortunately, our get-together wouldn't happen for another week. That seemed prudent since both of us would be busy dealing with the consequences of Mallory's murder at Catmmando Mountain.

What would I serve? While heating water for tea, I perused the cupboards and conducted a quick inventory. Miles stopped eating to snoop along with me. Soon bored by what he found, he resumed snacking. I struggled to fight off the ridiculous spell of anxiety that had gripped me as I stared at items on the shelves.

Was it the feelings Jack had stirred in me that had me riled up? Or the dreadful circumstances of the day?

Perhaps, a combination of the two. This situation wasn't the first one in which romance and murder had crossed my path, although it was premature to characterize my relationship with Jack as romantic. A little shudder of pleasure betrayed me. Dinner had been about more than business—deadly business. A different sort of shudder slinked down my backbone. I shut the cupboard doors and shifted my attention to Miles.

"Playtime," I announced as my tea steeped. Miles expects only a few minutes of fun from the feather teaser as part of our nightly routine, but he makes the most of it. The little guy can fly, leaping into the air in pursuit of those feathers. He gets all stealthy, too, as though the element of surprise gives him a better chance to catch his prey. I'm the one who's often surprised by a new trick in his display of feline prowess. He's a natural born clown, adding twists and turns, or Ninja yowls that make me laugh out loud.

Playtime over, I took my tea into the family room and watched the late edition of the local news. There we all were. Doug came across as tense, but he had stayed on message. Jack and I stood off to the side. The film crew had caught us both on tape. My eyes were fixed on Doug, willing him to hold it together, while Jack was watching me. I reacted with a flush of warmth at the frankness of his gaze captured in that unguarded moment.

The video clip ended, and the news anchors wrapped up the story. Late in the day, Mallory's name had been released to the public. Max had gone into seclusion, thank goodness. All in all, matters were under control—no more leaks and no public tantrums or gory photos. Not a word implied that I or anyone else at Marvelous Marley World had anything to do with the crime. A quick search on the Internet revealed much the same thing.

As I sipped my tea, I typed menu ideas for that dinner with Jack. Soon, I found myself going over the case, instead. I made a list of the names of the people we had spoken about at dinner, and then added Debbie Dinsmore, of all people, to that list. She seemed straightforward when she had calmed down enough to answer my questions. Still, what if there had been more to Purrsilla's meltdown than a reaction to stumbling upon that horrible murder scene? I'm sure Jack had considered that, but I'd mention it to him.

He should also have a chat with Megan Donnelly. She might know more about who Mallory was hassling at Snappy Treats. Megan might also be aware of other problems at eateries in Arcadia Park. What if Mallory had shown up early to do her job? Checking up on an issue at one of the Snappy Treats outlets, or another park restaurant, could be better handled before guests arrived. Had Mallory stumbled upon mischief that no one intended for her to see or reveal to others?

My mind raced with "what ifs" and whodunits. It cleared my head to write everything down. Who had leaked information about the incident before Doug and I arrived at the scene? I added names Doug had mentioned of people who were the first to find, report, and react to the incident.

Several colleagues who had tangled with Mallory at executive committee meetings came to mind, including a board member who had stormed out on one occasion. I added their names to my list.

During those stressful months I worked with Mallory in the Food and Beverage Division before moving to PR, there had been trouble. I'd dealt with several irate suppliers Mallory had insulted or angered by disregarding contractual arrangements. I struggled to recall their names and the nature of the disputes.

The task of listing potential suspects totally absorbed me. Miles had snuggled up against me when I sat down but disappeared at some point. He suddenly made his whereabouts known with a piercing yowl. I yelped in response and leaped to my feet, almost dropping my laptop in the process.

"What in the world?"

Miles flew to the large picture window in the room, stood on the back of an armchair, and poked his head through the drapes I'd drawn. Staring out into the darkness, he twitched his tail and began to growl. The fur on his back stood up, as did the hairs on the back of my neck. I slipped up behind Miles, trying not to startle him.

"What is it, Sweetie?" I peeked through an opening in the drapes and thought I saw movement outside. Garbage cans on the side of the house rattled as though someone had banged against them. My heart pounded. I was about to call 911 when a cat squalled and took off, with a second cat chasing him. Miles gave the glass in front of him a couple of "get out of here and stay out of here" smacks. Then he jumped down and began grooming himself. Crisis over. That was it for me, too. This day was over.

"Bedtime," I declared. Miles tore off. By the time I washed out my teacup and switched off the lights, Miles had turned in. He sleeps in the same cat bed he's had since he was a kitten. I've bought him bigger ones, but he has turned up his nose at them. I smiled at the furry little guy, rolled up into a ball and squeezed into his bed at the foot of my own. Why had I told Jack I live a solitary life?

7 NO BOY-TOY PHOTO

My sleep had been restless. The full impact of what had happened the day before, hit me like a ton of bricks after Miles woke me with a bellow. A successful wake-up call when delivered two inches from my ear. I don't know how he does it, but my cat always manages to go into rooster mode a minute or two before the alarm goes off. I hit the snooze button and closed my eyes. Would it be so terrible if I took a sick day? Miles was having none of it. When it's time to get up, you get up. He poked at my eyes with a soft paw and tickled my face with his whiskers until I gave in. I work for a cat at home, too.

"Oh, all right. Breakfast!" In a blur, Miles was gone. Ten seconds later he was yowling at me from the kitchen. Can I help it if humans are so much slower than felines? "I hear, and I obey," I shouted in reply as I dragged myself to the kitchen. He kept up a steady beat of calls, urging me on until I served him his breakfast. Blessed silence followed once Miles had his morning treats. Coffee, oatmeal, and fruit were on the menu for me. After the second cup of coffee, I managed to get through the rest of my morning routine, with Miles supervising, of course.

On the commute to work, I reviewed the day ahead. We had a full agenda, aimed at managing the murder at Catmmando Mountain crisis. That was in addition to more general outreach and engagement activities intended to put a friendly face on Marvelous Marley World Enterprises and support its internationally recognized brands.

Because of the theme park, we have teams involved in all sorts of local community events. Many events related to animal welfare, pet adoption, pet-owner education, and the like. A shared schedule keeps us all on the same page about who is doing what, when, and where, under normal conditions. Who knew what would happen, today? When I arrived at my office, Carol met me with more coffee—a hefty cup, freshly made.

"Bless you, Carol!"

"You're going to need it. You have a visitor. Linda Grey came in here upset, so I put her in your office."

"Has Jack spoken to you?"

"Ooh, Jack, is it? Chummy! I have an appointment with Detective Wheeler later. He's going to give me the third degree, right? Not that I'll mind too much. Meow! He's cute, unlike that oversized tomcat roaming the halls around here."

"I wouldn't call Jack cute." I frowned. How had our conversation wandered so far off topic?

"Don't worry, I know Rockford's only got eyes for you." She winked.

I blushed.

"Don't tease me." Jim Rockford— that was it! James Garner, in real life, was the name of the guy I couldn't come up with when I was trying to figure out who Jack resembled. I decided to steer the conversation back to business. "Did you put anyone in my office yesterday— or notice anyone else roaming the halls besides Dale?"

"No, I didn't put anyone in your office. Yes, I noticed people roaming around. This place is crawling with people all day long, Georgie. Yesterday was exceptionally busy with the uh... you know, with all that was going on with Mallory's, uh, demise. Dale was the only visitor in a character outfit, though. No Catmmando Tom sightings today, so far. I guess you gave him *'paws'* to reflect, eh? Made it *'purr-fectly'* clear you *'pre-fur'* the handsome detective?" I rolled my eyes.

"How much of this coffee have you had? Enough with the cat puns, already! You know I've heard all of them a million times before."

"I know. No need to be *'catty,'* I won't annoy you any *'furr-ther.'* I'm just trying to lighten things up before you go in there." She glanced down the hall toward my office.

"I hear you. Thanks for the coffee and the heads up."

In my office, I found Linda, sitting in obvious discomfort on the edge of a chair.

"I'm so glad to see you," I said. "Hang on a sec while I settle in, then we can talk."

"No problem." Linda's reply was a whisper.

I set my coffee down, hung up my coat, stashed my purse, and did a couple of other things while keeping an eye on Linda. She did not look well.

"Can I get you coffee or water?"

"Water would be great. My mouth is dry. Can you shut the door?"

"Sure." I shut the door and grabbed a bottle of water from a cabinet. As she opened that bottle, I sat down behind my desk. Trying to sound casual, I asked her, "What's up?" Her hand shook as she drank from the bottle.

"I'm worried about what's going to happen now that Mallory's dead." Tears slid down her cheeks. I pulled tissues from a box on a shelf behind me and handed them to her.

"Thanks. It's been so awful, ever since you left the Food and Beverage Division." A wave of guilt hit me. I felt the urge to apologize, but I didn't want to interrupt now that she had started to speak. When she sobbed instead, I spoke.

"I'm sorry. Will you tell me what you mean?" I smiled hoping to encourage her to open up.

"You know how Mallory was. Always nasty. Lately, she was on Dorothy's case, constantly. It's like she hated Dorothy. Maybe because Dorothy was so quiet and never stood up to her. Mallory said mean things, not only about Dorothy's work but about her appearance—her weight, her hair, her clothes—you name it! Sometimes Mallory even called her names like idiot or jerk and cursed at her. It was terrible, but what could I do?" Linda searched my face. I had to be displaying shock and horror since that's what I felt.

"I had no idea," I said. "Mallory was nasty while I was there, but she never resorted to name-calling or cursing. I am so sorry you had to endure that. Why didn't you or Dorothy come to me?"

"I wanted to, but Dorothy wouldn't let me. She said running to you would make it look like she couldn't handle her job. When I asked her about going to someone else, she told me to mind my own business. I tried. Since we're all in the same suite, I couldn't help hearing them, especially if they left the door to Mallory's office open. I considered going behind Dorothy's back to complain about Mallory. That would have been professional suicide, you know? Dorothy would be angry with me, and what would I do if Mallory came after me? I need this job, Georgie." Linda stopped talking and twisted the tissue in her hands.

"Linda, I am so sorry. Dorothy had a responsibility to be more responsive to your concerns. If you want to file a complaint, you can still do that. Mallory can't seek retribution now. I can understand if you've had it with Dorothy, too, and want to find another position in the Food and Beverage Division, or elsewhere. I'll help you. With Mallory gone, Dorothy's in charge. If you'd rather stay where you are, things should calm down."

"That's just it. Dorothy's gone off the deep end! I heard her shredding things yesterday and talking out loud to herself like there was someone in her office. I looked. There wasn't anyone in there. She was slamming things around and cursing under her breath about Mallory." Linda was trembling all over, as she continued.

"Georgie, I'm afraid Dorothy

might have had something to do with what happened to Mallory. You wouldn't believe the fight they had a few days ago. They had the door closed, but I could hear them shouting. Not just Mallory, but Dorothy, too. Then Dorothy stormed out, and Mallory came after her cursing and saying she was going to tell her dad to fire her." Linda squirmed in her seat.

"Dorothy told Mallory to go ahead, and she'd tell him what was going on. Mallory went back into her office and slammed her door."

"Going on? What *was* going on?"

"I'm not sure, but Dorothy knows. She was angry to find me sitting at my desk when she came out of there. I asked if I should call someone for help. Dorothy just pointed at me and said, 'Don't you dare! I've already told you to stay out of it.' So I did, but now it's too late."

"Have you told any of this to

Detective Wheeler?"

"Not yet. I'm supposed to talk to the police today. I wasn't sure I could do it with Dorothy standing there, or in the other room, you know, so I came to see you first? I heard the detective is going to be here later to do a press conference, right? Can you give him this, please? When I went in to water Mallory's plants this morning, I found it on the floor, shoved behind a potted plant near the door. I was going to put it on Mallory's desk, but then I thought it might mean something, so I came over here to give it to you. It shocked me a little to see them together like that. Do you think it's important?" I stared at the photo she handed me, stunned.

"It could be. We'll let Detective Wheeler decide. I'm sure he's going to want to speak to you, Linda. I don't believe you should go back to your office until we sort this out. Is there someone we can call to get you—a friend or family member?"

"Do you think Dorothy did it? Will she come after me next?"

"I don't know whether Dorothy had anything to do with Mallory's death or not, but her behavior is inappropriate. There's no reason for you to have to go through more distress than you already have."

"I'll call my friend, Nadia. It's her day off. She can pick me up, and I'll go home with her. You can call me at her place when Detective Wheeler wants to talk to me."

"That's a great idea. You call Nadia, and I'll call Detective Wheeler."

"I don't know what else I can tell the detective that I haven't already told you."

"He'll want to hear it from you directly—in case, I miss a point or get the details wrong. I'm grateful you've been willing to come forward about this. Jack Wheeler will be grateful, too."

Linda tried to smile as she pulled the phone from her purse and called her friend.

I tried to reach Jack but had no luck. I left a message several places and finally asked Carol to have him drop in when he arrived to interview her. Once Linda left, I plunged into tasks planned for the day.

When Jack returned my call later, I missed it. A few minutes before our scheduled meeting to prepare for the afternoon press conference, he zoomed into my office. I could swear I felt the air pressure change with that breezy entrance.

"Hey, Georgie, this has been quite a day. I got your messages, and I have questions for you." Jack dropped into the chair across from my desk.

Without even asking, I stood up and poured the man a cup of coffee. Usually, I use one of those little single cup doohickeys, but this was a coffee binge kind of day, so I'd made a whole pot.

"Great!" I said. "Did you find more incriminating evidence that puts me on your most wanted list?" A wry smile spread across his face, so much like James Garner!

"You're on my most wanted list, but it has nothing to do with this case."

"Oh, stop it. You're embarrassing me." I blushed for the second time today.

"Geez, don't tell me you don't like flirting any better than compliments."

"I like it. I just haven't had much practice lately with either."

"Stick with me, kid, and you'll get plenty of practice with both." He wore such a smug, determined expression it made me laugh. Not to mention he was using that hokey private eye voice again.

"Sure thing, but it'll take me a little time."

"Take all the time you need. I'm not going anywhere." His voice took on a more serious tone. He put both hands behind his head and stretched. "We only have a few minutes before our meeting. I guess we'd better get down to business. You go first."

"I suppose Carol told you I had a visit from Linda Grey. She's scared, and she's worried about Dorothy. You need to speak to Linda. See if you can help her sort things out." I quickly filled him in on the rest of our conversation. "Linda has no idea what Dorothy meant when she said she knew what was going on. I wonder if it has something to do with this." I handed him the photo Linda had given me earlier. Jack let out that low whistle he had used the day before when I suggested we dine at Blue Pacific.

"Mallory got around, didn't she? That's something I wanted to talk to you about—hanky-panky between Mallory and corporate associates. One reason Debbie Dinsmore and her friends disliked Mallory is that she stole their boyfriends. She collected boy-toys like Cruella went after those 101 Dalmatians. Megan Donnelly knew about it, too, apparently. Debbie Dinsmore says Megan became livid about all the trouble Mallory caused among park associates." Jack took another look at that person in that photo. "He's no boy-toy, though, is he?"

8 IDENTITY CRISIS

It was nearly dark when I reached my car. That's not unusual at this time of the year. It's often dark when I arrive at work and dark when I leave. Close by, I could hear a bicycle bell, one of those old-fashioned, pre-electronic-era bells that ring when you move a little lever. Max Marley loves them, and he's had bells installed on a fleet of bicycles that guests could use in Buddy Bear's Bicycle Bonanza. It is a rather pleasant sound—nostalgic, reminding me of riding with childhood friends at a furious pace through our suburban neighborhood.

I wasn't at all surprised by the sound. We have the same kind of bicycles here on the grounds of the World Headquarters complex. That includes the administrative building where I work, as well as Marvelous Marley Research & Development; Marvelous Marley Communications; Marvelous Max Studios; Marvelous Marley Foods; and several other buildings in the park-like campus.

I'd almost reached my car when I heard the sound again—louder this time. I turned around just in time to see Buddy Bear hurtling toward me on a company bicycle. The frozen smile on the character's face did not reassure me. I dashed around the front of my car to the driver's side and jumped inside, setting off the car alarm at the same time. Buddy Bear followed. As he came around the front of my car, still going at a good clip, I flung open my driver side door. He slammed on his brakes, but too late. The bike went one way and Buddy

Bear the other. In less than a minute, a Marvelous Marley World security team pulled up and jumped out. I hollered so they could hear me above the blaring car alarm.

"Buddy Bear tried to run me down on his bicycle. Don't let him get away. Call the police!" I was hopping mad as I shut off the car alarm. Not only because I'd come so close to being mowed down, but now I had an insurance claim to file. I couldn't wait to explain how my door had gotten dented by a rampaging, make-believe bear on a bike.

Buddy Bear sat up. He adjusted the lopsided furry head he wore and looked around. When he tried to stand, the larger of the two security guards tackled him. Bear and guard landed on the ground with a loud "oomph."

"Move another paw and my partner will zap you with his Taser, Buddy Bear." That was a statement I never imagined hearing. I climbed out and leaned against my car while waiting for a response from the police to the call security had made.

Thank goodness members of the press, who had been milling about earlier in the day, had left. We had orchestrated another briefing to satisfy their demand for news about the murder at Catmmando Mountain. As planned, Jack had participated, this time, confirming that Mallory Marley-Marston was indeed the victim. He assured the press that a thorough investigation was still underway, but police had no reason to suspect Arcadia Park's guests were in any danger.

Doug had wrapped up the event with a few words about the loss of a valued member of our corporate family. Then he delivered an emotional appeal for the press to respect the Marley family's privacy at this difficult time. If we were caught on video again, I bet it would reveal that Jack watched Doug this time, while I watched Jack. What had he learned by observing Doug?

I was disappointed that Jack hadn't tracked me down or called later in the day. Ridiculous, I know since he was running a murder investigation. Now that he had discovered evidence of Mallory's penchant for collecting men, the list of potential assailants had grown by leaps and bounds. As Jack had pointed out, many of the men must have had furious girlfriends or wives.

I urged him to ask Debbie and Megan more about that. They should be able to tell him which coworkers were upset by Mallory's behavior around their boyfriends. Megan had faced an almost untenable situation—caught between angry subordinates and a ruthlessly inappropriate superior who also happened to be the park owner's daughter. She should, at least, have kept records of the complaints from associates, even if she hadn't decided what to do about them.

Mallory's hunting grounds had extended beyond Arcadia Park. The men in Mallory's life now included my boss, Doug, their tryst captured in that photo Linda had found. Taken at an even pricier restaurant than the Blue Pacific, the place catered to celebrities. Paparazzi had snapped that particular picture of Mallory and Doug.

Someone in the media had added a caption: *"In recovery, Marvelous Marley's enterprising heiress eats! Who's the Mystery Man?"* From the way their fingers touched while toasting whatever they were celebrating, it appeared that dinner was about more than business. When one of the security guards removed Buddy Bear's fake head, I was jolted back into the present.

"Dale? Dale Kinkaid? Why on earth did you try to run me down?" I shook a finger at my coworker as if that would do a bit of good.

"I'd like to hear the answer to that question, too." We all turned to see Jack walking toward us.

"What are you doing here?"

"Carol said you had just left. She thought I might be able to catch you if I hustled to your parking spot. I have news, but it looks like you're facing a new situation of your own." He nodded at the half-man, half-bear sitting on the ground.

"You had it coming to you for being stuck up—a liar too! I saw you out with him last night," Dale whined.

"I'm a liar? What about? Were you spying on me?" I struggled to grasp what he was saying.

"You told me you don't date men you meet on the job. That was a lie. I caught you! Don't get yourself all worked up about it." Dale spoke with a sneer on his face.

"She doesn't have to get worked up about it. Leave that to me," said Jack.

"What's it to you, Detective? One date doesn't give you any claim on her."

"I don't have a claim on her, but guess what? As it turns out, the State of California has one on you, isn't that right, *Kyle*?" Jack turned from the unmasked bear toward me before he continued.

"Georgie, meet Kyle Kincaid. It looks like Buddy Bear here has an identity crisis. Dale is his brother's name. Kyle, here, is well-known to police all over the area—not just Orange County, but LA and Riverside Counties. You're not the first target of his *spying*. Sometimes his spying gets out of hand, doesn't it, Buddy Bear? I'm sure this latest incident will get the state to revoke his parole."

"Good grief, are you saying the guy's a Peeping Tom or a stalker?"

"A bit of both. Make that a lot of both. His brother is not happy that he stole his identity to get this job. His driver's license is a fake. We can add identity theft to Kyle's rap sheet now too, along with whatever the D.A. decides to charge him with for attempting to run you down." Jack shook his head. "Not the teddy bear type, is he?"

"No, and he's no Catmmando Tom, either. Max does not like his characters to be defamed or degraded. I would not be surprised if Max goes after him now, too." I thanked my lucky stars, once again, that the press had left for the day. Finding out Catmmando Tom was, in fact, a Peeping Tom would have been a hard story to keep under wraps. Thus far, out of respect or sympathy for Uncle Max, they had refrained from publishing sensational accounts of Mallory's death.

Then it hit me. What about all that noise outside my house last night?

"Did you follow me home last night, Kyle?"

"I've said all I have to say. Arrest me if you're going to do it. I want a lawyer, and I want to make a deal. I know plenty about what goes on around here. Nobody takes that no-dating-on-the-job policy seriously except you, Georgie." As he uttered those words, a police car drove up. Jack greeted the uniformed officers and then let the security guy with the Taser gun fill them in on Buddy Bear's escapades and his identity.

"Jack, you might want to send someone to go through my garbage. There's a chance Kyle was doing more than spying last night and left me another Valentine." I explained what had gone on outside my house the evening before. Jack called the police department right away and asked to have a team meet us at my house.

I glanced at Kyle. Cuffed, and sitting on the ground, he appeared harmless enough. It still gave me the creeps to think about him outside my home. Once I'd seen those cats run for it, I hadn't given the incident much more thought. My house is in a gated community, guards patrol the streets, and Jack had asked for extra police patrols. Despite having been nabbed by the police in the past for his behavior, Kyle must have some skills to have sneaked in and out of my community like that without detection.

A second look at Kyle in that Buddy Bear outfit made me smile. Whether he realized it or not, Kyle was in over his head this time. When Jack finished his call, I spoke loud enough for Kyle to hear.

"You know, taking Kyle into

custody is the best thing that could happen to him. He's toast when Max Marley finds out about this. Especially, if he had anything to do with his daughter's death or misleading authorities about the investigation of her murder. A smart guy would start talking and not stop until he had given you every bit of information he has about *what goes on around here.*" As the police picked him up off the ground and guided him to their patrol car, Kyle scowled at me.

"True enough," said Jack. "But does Buddy Bear strike you as a smart guy?"

"Not as smart as he thinks he is, that's for sure."

"You would not believe the trail of carnage that woman left in her wake over the years," Jack said a while later. We stood on my lawn in the illumination provided by exterior lighting. More light streamed from the windows of my house. Every light in the house was on.

"Mallory was in and out of rehab, racked up gambling debts, got arrested for drunk driving, and had assault charges filed against her—paparazzi, mostly. Her father has worked long and hard to get her under control and keep her out of prison." Jack scuffed the ground in disgust.

"Your boss is an idiot if he got caught in her web. Why would he put his marriage in jeopardy and risk his job for a fling with a woman like that?"

"I didn't know about Doug's involvement with Mallory or any trouble in his marriage. He never said a word to me about it."

It was my turn to scuff the ground a little. Shocked by new revelations about another colleague, I understood how Jack could find Doug's behavior disturbing. I wanted to call it a day, climb into bed, and pull the covers over my head.

Calling it a night wasn't possible under the circumstances. Jack and I had to wait while the criminal investigators finished poking around in my garbage, looking for evidence that Dale or Kyle—whoever he was—had left when prowling around my house the night before.

"Doug wouldn't be the first man to rely on the wrong part of his anatomy to make a decision about a woman, Jack."

"I guess so. She was a younger woman. Not my type, but some men go for model-thin. I suppose it didn't hurt that she was also filthy rich—or would be someday. Max kept Mallory on a short leash, given she often used money in stupid and illicit ways. Still, her salary plus an allowance from daddy put her in a higher pay grade than Doug's. From that photo, it looks as though she was wining and dining the man. An affair could explain why his wife left him several months ago."

I caught movement from the corner of my eye. Miles was pacing, perched inside on a windowsill. When I first introduced Jack, Miles had been friendly enough. The detective even got a welcome yowl—a different greeting altogether than the one Miles has for me when I return home.

However, when things didn't go as usual after that, and we disrupted his routine, Miles made it known he was not happy. Even with the windows closed, I could hear his bellows every occasionally. His tail switched as he watched us waiting for the criminal investigators to finish going through my trash. As bad as my job seemed to be at times, earning your keep by going through garbage had to be worse.

"The havoc continues even after Mallory's death," I said. "Poor Max will never be the same. Debbie Dinsmore and Linda Grey are both out of commission for a few days, at least. Heck, I may need time off, too, if another colleague turns out to be living a double life like Doug and Kyle. Or worse, if a bloodthirsty killer keeps planting evidence on me!"

"Well, Kyle has lawyered up. By tomorrow, if we don't come up with something to get him talking, the D.A. may offer that weasel a deal. I'm going to have another chat with your boss, too—tonight since I couldn't corner him in private earlier today. We'll see what Doug has to say about that photo. It's not looking good for him or Dorothy Sayers, for that matter. Neither of them has provided us with an alibi. Dorothy Sayers was a no-show for her interview today. After Linda Grey's revelations, I sent investigators to Ms. Sayer's house to pick her up and bring her in for questioning. No luck. Maybe she's making a run for it. We've issued an alert to watch for her plates and are checking for credit card charges in her name."

"That's not good, is it?" I asked.

Before he could answer, we heard a shout.

"Got something!"

We walked around to the side of the house. I was still wearing the red heels I'd chosen to go with my red dress. My shoes poked holes in the grass and got snagged on something. For a moment, I lost my balance. Jack reached out and grabbed my arm to steady me. *Snap, crackle, pop.*

"Sorry, I should have changed these shoes when we went inside."

He leaned in and whispered. "Nah, red is your color." Make that: *sizzle, sizzle, snap, crackle, pop.*

"What have you got?" Jack

hollered, as we approached a guy in a hazmat suit. The investigator said nothing, but he held up a wicked-looking boning knife.

"What do you want to bet that's our murder weapon, Georgie?" Jack asked as he shook his head in frustration.

"*Your* murder weapon—it's not mine!"

9 TGIF

I spent another night tossing and turning. Half asleep, I went over and over the people Jack and I had discussed. I racked my brain, rehashing recent interactions with Doug and Dorothy, Dale, who I now knew was really Kyle, Carol, and Linda. Even poor terrified Purrsilla, and her distressed supervisor Megan Donnelly. How had I missed the fact that one of them was capable of murder? These weren't strangers on the news, but colleagues and associates at a place where I felt safe, even when stressed out. One of the people I dealt with, perhaps on a daily basis, wanted to frame me for a horrendous murder.

The past two days had been two of the longest days I'd spent on earth. I could recall only one other time in my life that I'd felt so much like my world had turned upside down, overnight. Was that why this situation was getting to me? I stopped myself from thinking about that anymore. Sinking into the memories of that dark, dismal period in my past wouldn't help me cope with the current situation. It could even make matters worse, as I'd learned the hard way.

"TGIF," I whispered, as I rolled over and found myself eyeball to eyeball with Miles.

"Are you still mad at me?" His response was a prolonged "Yeow" as he took off down the hall toward the kitchen. I took that to mean our relationship was intact, routine reestablished. Miles had been in a snit by the time the criminal investigators hauled away my garbage, and I said goodnight to Jack. I spent a good half hour talking him down from his perch on top of the fridge. I resorted to bribery—tuna and peanut butter—two of his favorite treats. The peanut butter did it. I talked to him nonstop for the next twenty minutes and finally got a head bonk, followed by purring.

My ruminating about "whodunit" had started after that—even before I climbed into bed. It continued this morning. If I had to make a list of people who had it in for me, who would be on it? I struggled to recall the last time I'd had it out with anyone other than Mallory. No one came to mind before last night when I'd that row with Buddy Bear.

I'd given Dorothy high marks on her last performance review, which was another reason she'd been moved up into the position I vacated. Off the record, I'd suggested she continue to work on her people skills, and we'd identified several professional development options that might help her do that.

She'd displayed no hint of animosity toward me and even seemed to find our discussion helpful. Of course, that was no guarantee that she wasn't hiding resentment or other more negative feelings. Dorothy had apparently seethed long before she finally blew her stack at Mallory in that scene Linda had witnessed. Had she held similar angry feelings toward me and I missed them?

As I now knew, Doug had hidden plenty from me. Had he been pretending when he groused about Mallory, referred to her as "Worm-hearted," or commiserated with me about having to answer directly to her?

When had he and Mallory started their affair? I had to hand it to him, and to Mallory, too, for being able to conceal their personal relationship. Try as I might, I could not recall a single instance where I'd observed a hint of impropriety in their relationship—no flirting, furtive glances, or whispered confidences before or after a meeting.

I stewed all the way to work, still distracted when I arrived on my floor of the Marvelous Marley World administrative building that houses my office. I greeted Carol, accepted the coffee she offered and made my way down the hall to my corner office. Carol's updates barely registered.

When I sat down at my desk, I finally took in a few words she'd uttered to me in my inattentiveness. "...package on your desk, Georgie, along with your other mail." I couldn't remember how that sentence had started, but there it sat.

I hoped it wasn't another gift from Buddy Bear, aka Dale, aka Kyle. The large manila envelope had no postmark, so it had not gone through the postal system. It was taped in a sloppy manner, as though someone had been in a hurry when sealing it.

Should I open it or call Jack? I'd feel silly if he showed up at my office to watch me empty an envelope that contained fabric swatches or mock-ups of invitations for an event in the planning stages. I cut the top open and slid the contents out onto my desk.

What I found was an assortment of printed sheets from the Food and Beverage Division accounts, with specific items highlighted. Whoever sent them had attached invoices and receipts, too. It didn't take me more than five minutes to see what I was supposed to see. These were the kind of reports Dorothy and I'd reviewed for years. Had she sent them to me?

As I made my way through the stack of reports and attachments, the discrepancies were obvious—double-counted items, phony-looking invoices, and charges for items that were way out of line with what I would have expected to see. Tens of thousands of dollars out of line!

If I'd spotted any one of those problems, I would have insisted on a meeting with my superior, or taken them to the head honcho in Food and Beverage Management—the late Mallory Marley-Marston. Had Dorothy done that? Is that what had sparked the confrontation that Linda had witnessed? I picked up the business card Jack had left on my desk, punched in the numbers, and got his voice mail.

"Jack, I need to show you something. Can you..." I didn't get a chance to finish that sentence. A woman's hand reached out, pushed the button down on my phone, and ended my call.

"No need to tell your detective friend anything." Megan Donnelly stood there, pointing a gun at me. "You were clever to make a play for him. Fast too. At your age, it never occurred to me that you'd have that angle to work." The woman was wild-eyed and jumpy. Her hand that held the gun shook, with a twitchy finger on the trigger.

"You're still a winner, aren't you, with that million-dollar smile, perfect haircut, great figure, and a pricey wardrobe to show it off? That scarf should have been enough to land you in a jail cell instead of leaving you out and about to poke your nose into business that's not yours. I told Doug you'd be trouble. He was so sure he could keep you out of it by moving you to PR. Things were going fine, too, until that duo of freaks, Dorothy and Mallory went at it."

"What are you talking about, Megan?" Much of what she said was clear, although incredible. If I could only keep her talking, maybe I could come up with a plan to end this. Senior management and our staff all have panic buttons installed on our desks, but what if stampeding guards triggered a shooting spree? How could I get that gun out of her hands?

She must have caught me looking at that weapon.

"Stand up!" I did as she demanded.

"I don't have time to explain it to you," Megan said. "You're coming with me, now. No trouble! If you don't walk out of here wearing a gorgeous smile, people are going to die. Not just you, but Carol and a few others before I run out of bullets, or security stops me. What have I got to lose? Unless I can get you where we can stage our 'remorseful killer takes her own life' scene, this investigation won't end. I can't believe they found the murder weapon in your garbage, and you're still at your desk! That idiot Kyle is bound to start spilling his guts soon unless this ends today."

"You don't expect to get away with this, do you?" Clearly the woman was not all there if she thought my death would bring her troubles to an end.

Megan ignored the question. My hands brushed against the papers on my desk.

"I've been searching for those, by the way." She gestured with the gun toward the papers I'd reassembled into a pile.

"Shove them back in the envelope and give them to me."

I did as she requested, straightening the papers a bit before sliding them back into the envelope.

"Hurry up, will you?"

"Sure," I replied. When I looked up again, I noticed motion in the hallway outside my door. It was over in a split second. No sounds, either, but I glimpsed a pants leg worn by someone who was plastered flat against the wall.

I dropped my eyes, picked up the envelope, and thrust it abruptly toward Megan's outstretched hand. Megan startled at the sudden motion.

As she reached for the envelope, I drew it back a bit, so she had to lean in toward me, putting her at an awkward angle. At the same time, I picked up my still-steaming coffee and threw it at her hand that held the gun. The hot coffee slopped all over her as the mug hit her forearm. She yelped and dropped the gun.

I lobbed more missiles at her, using items on my desk. Megan shrieked as a heavy paperweight hit home. A stream of four-letter words followed, as she dropped to the floor and tried to retrieve that gun. Jack, a uniformed officer, and two members of our corporate security team stormed into the room.

"Don't make me shoot you, Ms. Donnelly. Leave that gun right where it is." Jack winked at me. "Nice going, Georgie. You handled yourself like a pro."

I plopped down into my chair before my legs gave way. I didn't feel like a pro, but I wasn't going to get into a tussle with Jack about paying me a compliment. Not now, maybe not ever again.

10 GANG OF THIEVES

A week later, Jack came to my house for dinner. Megan was on a suicide watch and was no longer talking. They had put a lot of the pieces together based on Megan's initial interview, as well as statements from Doug Addams, Kyle Kinkaid, and Dorothy Sayers. Doug, Megan, and Mallory were a gang of thieves.

Fortunately for me, before that awful confrontation in my office, police had found a partial print belonging to Kyle on the murder weapon. He squealed on Megan and the police sprang into action. When officers spotted her, and called in her location, Jack guessed she was going after me. He, his officers, and Marvelous Marley World security guards were in that hallway moments after she slipped into my office. The whole episode that began on Valentine's Day was mind-boggling.

"I know it's hard to believe. That's because you're not the scheming type. These three cooked up quite a little racket to scam old Max Marley. It's still not clear if Mallory needed the money, or if she just liked the idea of putting one over on dear old Dad."

"That poor man. He's got to be devastated to find out she did such a thing after all his kindness toward her. It must be hard for him to believe."

"I don't get her, either. Doug's easier to understand. His roving eye had him in trouble with his wife even before he took up with Mallory. He was in way over his head with financial difficulties, and a divorce was going to make that worse."

"Okay, so that just leaves Megan. What is her problem?"

"Megan was after more than money. For her it was about love, too. I wouldn't call what went on between her and your philandering boss love, but she did. Megan had oversight for park finances, so she played a crucial role in bilking the company by making up fake invoices to nonexistent suppliers and playing other tricks like that. The kind of thing you spotted right away when you went through the records Dorothy had delivered to your office. It's no wonder Doug wanted you out of there and helped you move to PR."

"Dorothy spotted the problems, too," I said.

"She did. Not right away, though. Dorothy was comparing this year's reports to last, when she discovered the accounting problems and dug out those invoices and receipts. She went to Megan, first, not realizing Megan was part of the problem. Megan blew her off, so Dorothy went to Mallory next. Mallory did more than blow her off. She started launching those nasty, personal attacks on Dorothy."

"That had to be awful for Dorothy."

"They meant it to be that way. Doug said he and Mallory thought they could force Dorothy out by making her life so miserable that she'd retire. She was about to hit you up for help when Mallory turned up dead. Dorothy freaked out, sent a copy of the documents to you, and got rid of everything else. I guess some of her threats directed at Mallory had become personal. As terrified as she was of becoming the next victim, Dorothy was also afraid of getting nailed as Mallory's killer. Dorothy's lucky she's not dead, considering how ruthless and unstable those three were."

"You're right about Dorothy's good luck. It sounds like they really underestimated her in many ways. Finding those accounting problems, threatening them, and refusing to resign despite all the abuse they were heaping on her must have put the three of them under increasing pressure. It's a little surprising they turned on each other instead of going after Dorothy."

"They were under pressure, all right. Megan, in particular, who was the weakest link in the chain of fools."

I sighed, hearing Jack use those words about a chain of fools. How could three seemingly reasonable people have gone off the deep end—together? Had Mallory's murder been more about "love-gone-wrong" than greed as some were claiming?

"The media has picked up on the idea that there was a classic love triangle behind all the Three-Musketeer comradery involved in their scam. Scamming each other too, I guess."

"That's about it. Doug and Mallory weren't fooling each other. Those two cutthroats were made for each other. It was a different story for Megan who was wrapped up in this wackadoodle fairytale. She thought she and Doug were headed for wedded bliss as soon as he dumped the current Mrs. Addams. That's before the picture surfaced of Doug and Mallory out on the town as a couple. She blamed Mallory, not her Prince Charming, for their deceit. When she's not considering suicide, Megan slides back into this movie running in her head. In it, Mallory is more Wicked Witch of the West than Cruella, and Megan is convinced she did the world a favor by killing her."

"I get it, but it's not like a house

dropped on her. She can't pretend it wasn't murder, can she?"

"Megan claims to be foggy about killing Mallory. According to Doug, it was Mallory's idea to meet in Arcadia Park, so it's not as though Megan lured her there. Mallory told Doug that Megan had found a way to skim more funds from the Snappy Treats outlets. Mallory wanted to see it for herself, so she set up the early morning meeting in a Snappy Treats kitchen. That's where Megan got the knife she used, although she says she doesn't remember taking it. She does admit they argued, not just about the fact that Mallory called her new idea stupid, but they also fought over Doug."

"Can you imagine the two of them fighting over him like that? That's soap opera material!"

"Mallory's whole life sounds like one big soap opera. A melodrama with a tragic ending. When Mallory stormed out in the middle of that argument, Megan followed her. She must have had that knife in hand, but Megan claims that's where the movie in her head fades to black. The coroner has filled in some of the blanks. It's not pretty, as you know."

"Do I want to hear this?"

"I won't go into all the gory details. That scrape Megan mentioned when she picked up Debbie Dinsmore didn't come from bumping her head on the golf cart. They examined Megan after that free-for-all in your office, and found cuts and bruises all over her body from the fight with Mallory. It was a vicious attack. Megan's still convinced that Doug is going to ride in on a big white horse and get her out of all the trouble she's in."

"That rescue fantasy never really grabbed me." I paused, searching for words. "At least not after...well, uh, not after I left my twenties behind."

Jack was staring at me with that penetrating, homicide investigator gaze of his. I could practically see the wheels turning in his head, wondering, no doubt, about what I'd left out of that last sentence. It was too soon to talk about it, even though murder and mayhem had stirred up unpleasant memories. I adjusted my oversized sunglasses and got the conversation moving again, in a different direction.

"So, did Megan find that photo or did Dorothy give it to her?"

"Neither, that was Kyle's handiwork. That creep was doing his thing, 'spying' on you and several of the women around you. When he got an inkling that something was going on between Doug and Megan, he decided to hit Doug up for blackmail money. He didn't have a bit of real evidence—just played the guy. Doug only made matters worse when he went straight to Mallory, with Kyle on his heels. Kyle did some more digging, found that photo on the Internet, and slid a copy under Mallory's door." I sucked in a breath of air.

"That has to be the one Linda found!"

"It must be. Kyle thought he could get on Megan's good side by sharing what he had found and took a copy of that photo to her. That sleazy Romeo planned to move in on her while she was off-kilter. He even told her about his blackmail scheme and offered to split the money they could make. Smooth, huh? That money was chump change compared to Megan's share of the take from the scam they were running. Kyle didn't know that. Nor did he realize she'd go after Mallory. When Megan went off the deep end the next day, she called Kyle in hysterics. She threatened to implicate him in the murder and paid him to plant the phone and the knife to frame you."

"I never saw Kyle put that phone in my coat pocket."

"The jerk was smug about that. He did it while you bent down to pick up papers he had knocked to the floor."

"That rat! He did shove things onto the floor when he slid that card and candy across my desk. How did Megan decide to pick me as the fall guy?"

"Megan admitted she never liked you. She made that clear while she had you pinned down in your office at gunpoint. Megan also admits to stealing your scarf, although that was done out of spite, not in anticipation of murdering Mallory and framing you. It was a small prize she took to get even with you and Mallory for fighting about it that day. After she killed Mallory, she ran and got your scarf and placed it at the scene."

"That fade-to-black part of the

movie in her head must have been over by then."

"Who knows how much of her claims of intermittent memory loss are true? Megan's undergoing a psychiatric examination. She seems pretty out of it, but I'm no shrink."

"Wow, I'm the one who was out of it! I knew Mallory was a problem, but I believed my relationships with my other colleagues were solid. I never dreamed I'd become a target."

"Your relationships with others made you a target," Jack said, "but also helped us crack this case. If Linda Grey and Dorothy Sayers hadn't trusted you, they might not have come forward as soon as they did. That wouldn't have put just you at risk, but others, too."

"Maybe so. I'm still stunned that I missed so much! I saw Dorothy and Linda often, even after I left the Food and Beverage Division. Why didn't they tell me what was going on?"

"Linda explained a lot of that. I'm convinced Dorothy didn't realize how much trouble she was in until it was too late. When Mallory was killed, she ran for it. Even then she trusted you with those documents she had delivered to you at your office." I sat in silence, hoping his words would sink in, and some light would go on.

"Can I pour you more wine?" I finally said. Jack nodded and held out his glass for a refill. "I'm sorry, but I still don't get what drives successful people like Mallory and Doug over the edge with their greed, or why Megan had it in for me."

"What don't you get? Even when you have a lot, there's always 'more.' And, why not you? Here we are sitting on this gorgeous patio of yours, overlooking the Pacific Ocean. We're drinking a fabulous bottle of wine that

Doug would no longer have been able to afford once his wife took him to the cleaners—unless their scheme paid off. Greed isn't always an easy thing to manage. Mallory had a ton of money but begrudged the fact you owned that designer scarf."

"Yes, I guess it's not enough for some people to just have more. They want it all."

"Exactly! As far as Megan's concerned, *you* have more than your share. You look like Jackie O. A woman who got better-looking as she aged, I might add. Megan was open in her resentment about your good looks and the fact that you had used them to take advantage of me." He smiled a wicked grin that I found irresistible.

"Oh, stop it. I wouldn't dream of doing such a thing, although I'll admit it might be fun to try. I doubt anyone could ever take advantage of a seasoned copper like you." He shrugged a little.

"I suppose we've had enough talk of people taking advantage of each other, haven't we?"

"Yes. It does sound like those three were stuck in a deadly race to the bitter end in their efforts to out-exploit each other and everyone around them, including me."

"Take greed, add envy and desperation and, voila, you've created a toxic cocktail. Do you really find it that hard to believe that people like that might find you intimidating, and even envy you a little?"

"Yes, I do," I replied slowly. "I'm at an age where more of my life is behind me than ahead of me. Money doesn't buy happiness, slow down the aging process, or keep trouble away. I don't have a husband or children, and my career's coming to a close."

"Whoa! Wait! I doubt that. Marvelous Marley World Enterprises just lost three key execs. The biggest problem you're going to face is which position to fill as you move up the ladder. Despite all the hoopla about youth, it's mature folks like us who run things. Unless you want to retire, I'd say there's another decade or more for you at the Cat Factory, right?"

"Yes, although after this week another decade sounds like an eternity. You're right, of course." I smiled as Jack went on with his pep talk.

"As for kids, I'll bet Max Marley might have a bone-weary word or two for you about having chosen the path of parenthood. That just leaves the husband issue. Who knows? Maybe there's some guy around who thinks it's a miracle you're single. Could be he's a little intimidated, too, but so bedazzled he was willing to make a fool of himself by asking you to dinner, even in the middle of a homicide investigation." Those brown eyes mirrored the earnestness in his words. I took the hand he offered and smiled. *Snap, crackle, pop!*

~~~~~~

Thanks for reading Murder at Catmmando Mountain. I hope you enjoyed meeting Georgie Shaw, Jack Wheeler, and Miles. Please take a few moments to leave a review for me on AMAZON and GOODREADS. Join me at my website: http://www.desertcitiesmystery.com

Sign up for my newsletter & you'll get news, giveaways, blog posts, and recipes. You'll find **recipes from this book below**!

There's more murder and mayhem in store for Georgie Shaw and Detective Jack Wheeler! Find all the books in the series at: http://bit.ly/georgie5. Coming soon, Murder of the Maestro, Georgie Shaw Cozy Mystery #6.

A new mystery brought them together. Will an old one drive them apart? Up next, it's an excerpt from ***Love Notes in the Key of Sea***: Georgie Shaw Cozy Mystery #2.

LOVE NOTES IN THE KEY OF SEA
1 ALARMING NEWS: AN EXCERPT

"Jack, there's been a murder!" Jack and I had been sitting on my patio, taking in the view of the Pacific Ocean when my phone rang. Summer was well on its way, here, on the Southern California Coast in June. Still, a chill hung in the air as the sun sank toward the horizon. The chill I felt wasn't entirely due to the weather. Before I could say more, Jack jumped to his feet and pulled his phone out of the pocket of his jeans.

"I don't see a message. Why would someone from the department call me on your landline?"

"They didn't. The murder's not here. It's on a beach somewhere in North Carolina near where Jennifer Dodson's daughter has been going to school. Someone attacked Meredith on the beach."

"No, Georgie! Are you saying someone murdered Jennifer's kid?"

"No, Meredith's not dead, but a man stabbed her, and she's recovering in the hospital. Jennifer flew out there a couple of days ago. She didn't call me until she was sure

Meredith was going to be alright. There have been a series of attacks at the beach—all women. Meredith was fortunate, apparently, since she lived through the assault. Another woman attacked in a separate incident died. The next night a third attack occurred. Kat Benson, a graduate student in art history at UNC Chapel Hill, attends the same school where Meredith's enrolled. She's not dead, but not doing well."

"Did Meredith know both other women?" I could tell I'd triggered Jack's detective side and had set his inquisitive mind in motion.

"Kat yes, but not the woman murdered on the first night—Jenna somebody—I don't remember her last name. Kat was a graduate assistant for an undergrad art history course Meredith took. I guess they hit it off and became friends. Meredith was distraught when the police questioned her and grew even more upset when told someone had attacked her friend, too. Meredith's scared."

"Who could blame her? It's hard to feel safe when something horrific like that happens."

"The police have the attacker, but

Jennifer's not convinced it's safe for Meredith, either, so she plans to bring her home as soon as she can. I hate to change our plans for the weekend, Jack, but I'm going to visit Jennifer and Meredith when they get home. Jennifer seems to think it would be good for me to be there because..." It's as though something suddenly swallowed me up and I couldn't finish that sentence.

"Because you went through something similar at Meredith's age. What exactly, I don't know, do I? Every time the subject comes up, you slip away, then go silent. It's like a ghost story. Only the ghost is the part of you that steals away to Corsario Cove whenever something sets off your memories of that event. You're otherwise one of the smartest, most with-it women I've ever met, and yet you carry this secret around with you like Marley's chain. Not your boss Marley, but that ghost in the Dickens Christmas story. I... I'm going to shut up. We've been through this before, and I don't want to make you feel worse since you're obviously upset. When you're ready to talk, I'm here."

"I am having this déjà vu experience. I don't always know what will trigger it, but news about a murder on the beach has set it off, big time."

I stared at the new man in my life, trying to figure out why I couldn't say more. Jack Wheeler's the first man I've been this close to in years. No, make it decades. I'm not talking about a mere flirtation with the handsome homicide detective—a Jim Rockford lookalike. Not a fling, either. There had been other men since that horrendous incident in Corsario Cove changed my life forever. Since then, I'd learned that attraction may be instantaneous, but not love. None of the men I met after losing Danny had me contemplating love and marriage—until Jack. The more I thought about making a serious commitment, though, the more all the old memories hounded me.

"I want to tell you what happened. I should have done it already. It's just..." Jack took a step forward and pulled me into his arms.

~~~~~

Read the rest of mystery #2, **Love Notes in the Key of Sea**, as a stand-alone eBook on AMAZON KINDLE or as part of the boxset, Georgie Shaw Cozy Mystery Series: Novellas 1-3 @ http://bit.ly/Shawboxset. Find all the books in the series @

http://bit.ly/georgie5. I hope you'll also check out the books in two other mystery series I write.

The Jessica Huntington Desert Cities Mystery series @ http://bit.ly/JessHunt4 is set in the desert near Palm Springs. The series features a rich, shopaholic thirty-something lawyer and amateur sleuth. Jessica Huntington who gets a wake-up call about the mess her life has become when her best friend's husband turns up dead.

I hope you'll check out all the books in this series:

A DEAD HUSBAND
A DEAD SISTER
A DEAD DAUGHTER
A DEAD MOTHER
A DEAD COUSIN—out 2018

The prequel to the Jessica Huntington series is also available: ***Love a Foot Above the Ground*** http://smarturl.it/loveabove.

The Corsario Cove Cozy Mystery Series featuring twenty-something newlyweds, Kim and Brien. Two characters from the Jessica Huntington series, the surfer dude pool boy turned security guard, Brien Williams, who teams up with the sarcastic, street-wise survivor, Kim Reed. Together they're in for all sorts of hijinks that take place on California's Central Coast. The swanky Sanctuary Resort and Spa at Corsario Cove is the perfect setting for holidays and special occasions except for the fact that a surprising number of mysteries unfold there...some new and some that reach into the distant past. Available on Nook, iTunes, & Kobo as well as Kindle.

COWABUNGA CHRISTMAS! Corsario Cove Cozy Mystery #1
https://books2read.com/u/mdKPlX
GNARLY NEW YEAR! Corsario Cove Cozy Mystery #2
https://books2read.com/u/b6Q7x6
HEINOUS HABITS! Corsario Cove Cozy Mystery #3
https://books2read.com/u/bWZrqD
COMING SOON: *RADICAL REGATTA! Corsario Cove Cozy Mystery #4*

Before you go on to finish reading book two, here are a few of Georgie Shaw's favorite recipes. They're taken from some of the delicious items featured in *Murder at Catmmando Mountain.*

ENJOY!

RECIPES

Flourless Chocolate Cake*

Ingredients

- 1 pound semisweet chocolate bar, chopped
- 1 cup (2 sticks) unsalted butter
- 1/4 cup coffee liqueur
- 1 teaspoon vanilla extract
- 7 large eggs, room temperature
- 1 cup sugar
- Powdered sugar

Preparation

1. Preheat oven to 350°F. Butter 9-inch-diameter spring form pan with 2 3/4-inch-high sides. Line bottom of pan with parchment paper. Stir chocolate, butter, coffee liqueur, and vanilla in heavy large saucepan over low heat until melted and smooth. Cool to lukewarm.

2. Using electric mixer, beat eggs and 1 cup sugar in large bowl until thick and pale, and slowly dissolving ribbon forms when beaters are lifted, about 6 minutes. Fold 1/3 of egg mixture into lukewarm chocolate mixture.

Fold remaining egg mixture into chocolate mixture.

3. Place prepared pan on baking sheet. Transfer batter to prepared pan. Bake until tester inserted into center comes out with moist crumbs attached, about 55 minutes. Cool 5 minutes. Gently press down edges of cake. Cool completely in pan. Cake can be prepared up to 1 day ahead. Cover with plastic wrap and refrigerate. Let stand at room temperature 1 hour before continuing.

4. Run knife around pan sides to loosen cake. Remove sides of pan; transfer cake to platter. Remove parchment paper. Sprinkle cake with powdered sugar and serve. 12 Servings

*from Cafe Mundo San Jos Costa Rica

Prawn Cocktail with Marie Rose Sauce*

Ingredients

- Lemon juice, to taste
- Salt, to taste
- 20 x raw tiger prawns, shells on
- 1 small head butterleaf lettuce
- cayenne pepper, to serve

For the sauce

- 1/2 lemon, juice only
- 1 tablespoon Worcestershire sauce
- 5 tablespoons tomato ketchup
- few drops Tabasco sauce
- 2 pinches smoked paprika
- 1/2 teaspoon paprika
- 1 tablespoon double cream
- 4 tablespoons mayonnaise
- 1 pinch cayenne pepper
- pinch salt
- 1 tsp cracked black pepper

Preparation

1. Bring a large pan of water to a boil. Add a squeeze of lemon and salt. Add the whole prawns and cook until they rise to the surface. Drain and chill in ice-cold water.
2. Peel the cooled prawns, leaving one prawn unpeeled (for the garnish).
3. Cut the head of lettuce in half and rinse.
4. For the sauce, mix all the sauce ingredients together.
5. To assemble the cocktails, drain the lettuce and pat dry with kitchen paper. Arrange a few lettuce leaves, lining martini glasses or small bowls. Shred the remaining leaves and toss with the peeled prawns and sauce. Top with the unpeeled prawn and a sprinkling of cayenne pepper. 4 Servings

*from Master Chef John Torode featured on BBC website

Mushroom Crusted Chilean Sea Bass*

Ingredients

- 7-ounce fillet of Chilean sea bass
- 6 ounces dried porcini mushrooms
- 8 ounces white mushroom — rinsed and sliced
- 8 ounces Portobello mushroom — sliced
- 3 cloves garlic
- 2 tablespoon softened butter
- 2 ounces fresh basil leaves chopped
- 1 cup white unseasoned panko crumbs
- salt and pepper to taste
- spring onions or leeks, thinly sliced, for garnish

Directions

1. Soak dried porcini mushrooms in enough hot water to just cover when submerged — 'til softened. Place soaked mushrooms with its liquid, white mushrooms, and Portobello mushrooms in a pot and bring to a boil.

2. Lower flame to a simmer, add butter, a tsp of salt & pepper — stir to incorporate butter and liquids with salt and pepper. Cook

for about 30 minutes on a low flame — watch to make sure the liquids do not evaporate all the way, add water if necessary.

3. Remove from stove top, let cool to room temperature. Remove excess liquid and set aside. Place mushroom mixture in a food processor and blend till smooth, adding the liquid set aside as needed to keep it a smooth texture.

4. Now add the freshly chopped basil and continue to process. Once all ingredients are blended well, add unseasoned panko crumbs — this will firm up the crust. Season with sea salt and freshly ground pepper. Heat a cast iron skillet with 1 tsp olive oil and sear the fish on both sides for about 2 to 3 minutes. Remove from stove top and coat top of fish with the mushroom mixture about 1/4 inch. Place in preheated 400° oven for 10 minutes until fish flakes.

5. Fry thinly sliced leeks and place on top of crust to garnish. 1 serving

*from Albert A Bijou, Executive Chef at The Coffee Bar, a much-heralded Kosher restaurant in Lawrence, New York

ABOUT THE AUTHOR

I'm an award-winning, USA Today bestselling author who enjoys *snooping into life's mysteries with fun, fiction, & food—California style!*

Life is an extravaganza! Figuring out how to hang tough and make the most of the wild ride is the challenge. On my way to Oahu, to join the rock musician and high school drop-out I had married in Tijuana, I was nabbed as a runaway. Eventually, the police let me go, but the rock band broke up. Our next stop: Disney World, where we "worked for the Mouse" as chefs, courtesy of Walt Disney World University Chef's School. More education landed us in academia at The Ohio State University. For decades, I researched, wrote, and taught a number of gloriously nerdy topics. Retired now, I'm still married to the same, sweet, guy and live with him near Palm Springs, California. I write mysteries set in sunny California! The Jessica Huntington Desert Cities Mystery series set here in the Coachella Valley and the Corsario Cove Cozy Mystery Series set in California's Central Coast, The Georgie Shaw Mystery series set in Orange County—better known as the OC.

Join me at: http://www.desertcitiesmystery.com

Made in the USA
Middletown, DE
14 October 2022